Igniting the Flame

Zoe Piper

Published by Apollo8 Publishing

Cover design: Designs by Morningstar

Professional Beta Reader: Leslie Copeland, LesCourt Author Services

Editing: Jenni Lea, Proof Your Love

Proofreading: C Beehre

ISBN: 978-0-473-50264-5

Acknowledgements

Thank you, as always, to you, for taking the time to read my book. If you'd like to leave a short review it would be appreciated as reviews help authors in all sorts of ways.

This book was hard to write. After 'talking' to me all through books one and two, Brett and Stuart went quiet when it came to their story. I owe a huge thank you to Jay Hogan for many things, including alpha reading when I got so tied up and didn't know where I was going, for encouraging me when the self-doubt set in, and for letting me have Reuben and Cam from *Crossing the Touchline* pop into The Smoking Keg for a drink! (Go read her *Auckland Med* series, you won't be disappointed).

Leslie Copeland gets mentioned by so many authors for her skill as a beta reader and she is truly a gem in this crazy publishing world. She pulls no punches and if something is not working, she'll tell you. Thank you Leslie for helping me make this so much better than it started out.

To Morningstar Ashley for distracting me from my muggle job by sending pictures of hot fireman. I think we got the right one! Love you and your work.

Christine C and Jackie C for beta reading. As always, your feedback and support means so much to me.

Editor Jenni Lea for bashing this into shape. It was a mess before you started and the polish is all yours.

Corrinne for proofreading. As always, anything that has slipped through is my fault, not yours.

A special thank you to Elena James for coming up with the title.

To friends and family – yep, I'm still doing this writing thing.

Also by

Prologue

Eighteen years ago

"That was a great shot on goal tonight," Stu said to his best friend as they meandered home after their weekly summer soccer game. He lazily dribbled the ball along the pavement, causing it to skitter and jump before Brett expertly caught it with his foot.

"I know," Brett said with a laugh. "Did you see the look on Harrison's face when it flew past him?"

"I did. He was totally not paying attention to the game."

"Yeah, he was checking out Lara on the girls' team." Brett kicked the ball ahead of them. "Can't say I blame him though. She's pretty hot."

Stu hummed and dropped his gaze to the path in front in them, a pang of jealousy going through him as Brett continued to rave about the merits of Lara Jones. He kicked at a loose stone, watching it bounce off the kerb. He really didn't want to hear how long Lara's legs looked in her soccer shorts. His attention had discreetly been on the strong muscles in his best friend's legs.

The sound of a car speeding towards them had Stu looking up just as a head poked out of the open passenger window and *"faggots"* was yelled, followed by raucous laughter. Brett responded by giving the fingers to the retreating car.

"They're the faggots," Brett muttered as he snatched up the discarded soccer ball.

Stu picked up his pace, pulling the strap of his training bag tighter onto his shoulder.

"Hey, Stu. Wait up. What's the rush?"

"Oh, nothing. Just need to get home," Stu said, not slowing his pace.

"Oi, idiot. Did you forget you're coming back to mine for dinner before I whip your arse at *FIFA*?" When Stu didn't reply, Brett grabbed his arm, halting him. "Mate. What's up?"

"Nothing," he said, shaking his head.

"Then why are you going home to an empty house? You know Mum will have cooked dinner for you. She always does on a Tuesday."

Stu's stomach churned. It was getting harder to hide his secret, especially from his best friend. The thought of not having Brett in his life had kept his mouth shut.

"Stu, come on, mate. What's wrong? Is someone bullying you at that fancy pants school?"

Screwing up his courage, he took a long look at his friend. It may be the last time he could do so openly. Brett was an inch or so taller than him, long limbed with big hands he still had to grow into. His blond hair was mussed and damp from their soccer game and his blue eyes were staring back at Stu with concern.

"Those guys, in that car," Stu said, nodding down the road. "They were right."

"Huh?" Brett squinted in the direction the car had gone.

"When they called out. They were right. I am."

"You are what?" Brett asked, confusion written all over his face.

The situation was almost comical, and Stu chuckled mirthlessly. He couldn't even come out properly.

"I'm gay, B. When they called out faggot, they were right."

Stu studied his friend carefully, watching for his reaction. Brett's eyes widened slowly as realisation dawned and then he slowly scanned him from top to toe.

Stu resisted the urge to wrap his arms around himself, to hide away.

"Huh. Okay then," Brett said, dropping the soccer ball and dribbling it as he began walking again. Stu didn't move from his spot, unsure of what to do next. Brett glanced over his shoulder. "Well, are you coming or not? Mum's making her world-famous chicken."

"Y-you still want me to come over?" Stu stammered out.

"Yeah, of course. Why wouldn't I?"

"Brett. I just told you I'm gay. You sure you still want to be friends with me?" Stu managed to hold his voice steady as he asked the one question he wasn't sure he wanted to hear the answer to.

"Why wouldn't I want to be friends with you? So you're gay. So what?" Brett rolled his eyes and turned to walk away.

Hope flared in Stu and tension eased from his body as he slowly followed his friend. Brett nudged him in the ribs as he drew level.

"Gay, huh? How long have you known?" Brett's tone was curious, but Stu could see that his friend wasn't being mean.

"A little while. I...I told Mum and Dad on the weekend."

"Oh God." Brett groaned. "How did that go?"

"They were surprisingly okay with it." Stu huffed out a laugh. "They were more concerned with how I'd done on my English test and what subjects I'm looking at doing next year."

"Seriously? Well, that doesn't surprise me, God forbid you don't choose the right subjects and let down the Johnson name," Brett told him as they drew up to the front of his house.

"Thanks for taking it so well," Stu rushed out.

"Were you that worried I wouldn't?"

Stu gave a small nod, biting his lip in embarrassment.

"Mate, it really doesn't worry me who you fancy. You're a good person, and that's all that matters," Brett said. "Besides, it means more girls for me now."

"Yeah, 'cos they're just queueing up to date the great Brett Parker." Stu put a hand to his brow and scanned the empty street. "Oh look, is that someone there? Wait. No. They've turned the other way." He dropped his hand. "Sorry, B, looks like you've missed out again."

"Fuck off, Stu." Brett pushed him, a playful grin teasing the corners of his mouth.

"Brett Dean Parker! Don't swear!" Rose Parker's voice echoed from the house.

They both laughed and, pushing and shoving each other, raced for the door.

"Honestly, you two," Rose admonished as they tumbled into the kitchen. "Go and wash your hands and then come and have dinner before it gets cold."

Once they were at the table, Rose asked them about their game, smiling proudly when Brett told her about the goal he scored. She winked at Stu. "Did he do his usual victory dance?"

"Yup! Waved his arms around and did this fancy little jiggle on the spot," Stu told her, laughing as Brett glared at him.

"So, Mum. Just so you know, Stu's gay," Brett calmly stated before taking a mouthful of his dinner.

Stu froze, his appetite disappearing. He kicked Brett under the table and then chanced a glance at Rose. A thunderous look was on her face, and Stu carefully put down his knife and fork and began easing his chair back from the table.

"Thanks for dinner, Mrs Parker," he whispered, trying to hold back his tears.

"Sit right down, Stuart." She held him in his seat with a gentle hand on his shoulder. "Brett, you apologise right this instant," she growled at her son.

Brett flushed at his mother's tone and glanced at Stu. "Wha…what did I do?" he asked, eyes flicking between his mother and friend.

"Honestly, Brett. That was not your news to tell. It's up to Stuart who he tells and when. It's deeply personal. You're lucky it was me you blurted it out to and not some person who could hurt Stuart—and you, for that matter."

Horror crossed Brett's face and he reached a hand across the table to Stu. "Mate. I'm sorry. I didn't even think. You know I didn't say it to be mean, don't you?"

"It's okay, B. I know you engaged mouth before brain, like usual." Stu shoved his hands into his lap to hide their shaking.

A warm arm wrapped around his shoulders as Rose gently hugged him. "Stuart, you know you are always welcome here. You are always safe here, okay?"

"Thanks, Rose. That means a lot to me. Do…do you think John will be okay with it…me?" Stu asked, referring to Brett's father.

"John will be fine, honey. One of the managers at his work is gay and has a lovely boyfriend. John has a lot of respect for him, so don't you worry about a thing." She nodded at his plate. "Now finish up your dinner so you can beat my son at whatever game you're playing on the Xbox tonight."

Relief settled into Stu's bones. He'd been worried about Brett's reaction and if he'd still be welcome at his home. Brett's parents meant a lot to him, providing the warmth and emotional support his own parents lacked, both being busy with their careers.

The biggest hurdle had been crossed. Now all he had to do was get over the crush he had on his best friend, and life would be great.

Chapter One

Present day

Brett woke with a heavy, vibrating weight at the small of his back. It acted as a counterpoint to the drum solo being performed in his head and a mouth as dry as the Sahara Desert.

He reached behind him and his hand was butted by the cat making itself comfortable on the top of his arse. He cracked an eyelid, giving a low groan when the morning light hit his retina. Craning his head, he met unblinking yellow eyes.

"Hey, Bucky," he croaked out. Bucky blinked once before licking a paw and swiping at his ear. With a baleful glare, he settled back into the curve of Brett's lower back, a gentle purr rumbling through him. Not having the energy to argue, Brett buried his face in the pillow before his pounding brain caught up with the fact he was in a bed. Normally when he woke up with the judgemental cat on his back, he was on the very comfortable couch in his best friend's living room, *not* in his best friend's bed.

He gingerly swung his head to the other side of the wide bed but found it empty, the rumpled sheets and a dent in the pillow showing that someone had been next to him.

"Looking for me?" a decidedly too-cheerful voice asked.

Brett groaned and turned towards the sound, wincing. A pair of dark blue boxer briefs came into view, fitting snugly round a good-sized bulge.

"Fuck, mate. That's a sight I *really* don't need to see this morning," he complained, closing his eyes again.

"Aww, why not? There are plenty of guys who have enjoyed waking up to the sight of my junk," Stuart replied with a chuckle.

"I'm sure there are." Brett risked opening his eyes to find that Stuart had crouched down and was now eye-level. "However, as impressive a sight as it is..." his voice trailed off at the shit-eating grin Stuart was giving him.

"It is impressive, glad you noticed," Stuart teased, his blue eyes sparkling with amusement.

"Fuck off." Brett groaned, dropping face first back into the pillow.

"Is that anyway to talk to the person who has brought you Nurofen?"

"If there is coffee with it, then you're forgiven for waving your dick in my face," Brett told him, his voice muffled.

He heard Stu mutter something about him being so lucky as he felt the weight of Bucky being removed from his back. He rolled over, pushing himself up in the bed. Stu had the cat cuddled in his arms, petting the purring animal. "I don't think Uncle B is feeling too well, Bucky." He returned his attention to Brett. "Drink your Berocca and take your pills. While you're in the shower I'll make you a coffee."

Brett reached for the fizzing neon-orange vitamin drink and the two capsules from the bedside table. He threw the tablets in his mouth and drained the glass.

"Thanks, mate."

"You're welcome." Stu let a squirming Bucky go before crossing to the chest of drawers in the corner.

"Hey, why am in here and not on the couch?"

Stuart gave him a wicked grin over his shoulder. "Simple. You refused to sleep anywhere else." Opening a drawer, he pulled out a pair of old, faded jeans and wriggled into them before grabbing an equally faded blue sweatshirt.

Brett thought back to the night before. It had started out as beer, pizza, and watching the game with their friends. It had ended with friendly insults and… "Oh god. Whisky. You know I get a headache when I drink whisky. Why'd you let me have that shit?" he whined.

Stuart chuckled at his distress. "I tried to stop you, but you were adamant you'd be fine."

"Yeah, well, next time don't listen." Throwing back the covers, he sat on the side of the bed. "Still doesn't explain why I'm in your bed though."

Stuart paused by the door. "Charlie passed out on the couch, Jase and Kyle took the spare room, and although I offered to make up the air mattress, you said you'd share with me." He shrugged. "So, you did."

As Stuart recounted the events of last night, vague memories filtered back into his whisky-numbed brain. They'd had a nightcap, which had turned into several. Charlie had crashed out where he sat and as the only couple there, it had made sense for Jase and Kyle to take the queen-sized bed in the spare room. That had left the air mattress or Stu's bed.

Brett racked his brain as to why he'd insisted on sharing with Stu. He remembered that sorting out the air bed had seemed like too much effort. He glanced again at the rumpled covers and pillow. It looked like he'd stayed on his side of the mattress, which was a relief. His ex-girlfriend used to complain how snuggly he got when he'd been drinking and the last thing he wanted to do was make Stu feel awkward.

"It's okay, B, you were a perfect gentleman," Stu told him with a smirk. "As was I." With a sassy wink, his best friend left the room before Brett could figure out a reply.

Stretching his arms above his head to relieve the kinks in his back, he took a deep breath. Drinking whisky last night had been a mistake. He knew exactly what effect it had on him, and Stu's well stocked liquor cabinet had more than one alternative for him to choose from, but he'd chosen to drink what the others were drinking. He'd wanted the warm buzz and mellow feelings that came with drinking whisky. Just for a little while he'd wanted to chase away the hollowness that had recently taken up residence in his soul.

Pushing the melancholy thoughts away, he picked up his discarded jeans and t-shirt from the floor and made his way to the spacious bathroom with its large tiled walk-in shower, offset with an antique-style claw foot bath and pedestal sink unit.

Stuart lived in what had been an old, run down 1920s workingman's cottage when he bought it ten years ago. He had renovated the tired building, creating a modern, open airy home but had remained sympathetic to the era of the house.

Brett opened one of the wooden cabinets and pulled out a fresh towel and his toiletry bag. He'd stayed there enough times it had been easier to leave some of his personal soap and shampoo than always using Stu's.

Fifteen minutes later his headache had reduced to a dull throb and the smell of brewing coffee mingled with the scent of bacon frying had him heading to the kitchen where he found Stu busy at the stove.

He made himself a much-needed coffee and leaned against the island bench, sipping from his mug. Stuart hummed to himself as he flitted between the stove top and fridge, pulling eggs and cheese out.

"Want a hand?" Brett offered.

Stu shook his head. "Not with the food, but you can set the table if you like."

He quickly organised the cutlery and plates, as familiar with the kitchen as his own. He glanced up as Charlie shuffled into the room, hair damp from his own shower.

"Morning, mate. How's the head?" he asked with a grin.

"Better than yours," Charlie replied as he made his own coffee. "I don't suffer on whisky like you do."

"You crashed before me though," Brett pointed out.

"Haven't been sleeping much lately. The drink tipped me over the edge." Charlie dropped into a chair at the table. "And that couch is so comfy."

"How long before Cooper's home?" Stu asked sympathetically.

"About three more weeks. End of the month, all being good." Charlie smiled softly as he thought about his rock star boyfriend. "He's leaving London next weekend and doing two week's promotional work across the States and then he'll be here."

"For good this time?" Brett asked.

A bigger smile lit Charlie's face. "Yeah. For good this time. At least until he starts the tour for the new album. But this will be home now, rather than the UK or LA."

"So then you'll be getting even less sleep?" Stuart teased as he plated up the food.

Charlie grinned and winked. "Sounds about right."

"What sounds about right?" Jase asked as he and his boyfriend, Kyle, joined them.

"Glad you two could join us. Finished defiling my shower, have you?" Stuart said, raising an eyebrow.

"What? You let me shower after them?" Brett protested. "You could have warned me, mate."

"Relax, Parker. We didn't do anything," Jase reassured him. "And if we had, it's nothing to whatever Stu's done in there."

"He's right. There's a reason I made sure I had a large walk-in shower put in when I renovated."

Brett gave a mock shudder and groan as he took a seat at the table. "TMI, guys."

Stuart nudged his shoulder as he sat next to him. "Like you don't talk about your exploits with the blokes at the station."

"I don't have any exploits to talk about. Not lately anyway," Brett said as he piled food onto his plate.

"What about that nurse? Didn't you go out with her a couple of times?" Charlie asked.

"I did. She was nice enough, but that was weeks ago."

"Why haven't you seen her since?" Stuart asked with a frown.

"With her shifts and mine, it was too hard to schedule, and, to be honest, I wasn't feeling it." He gave a shrug and took another mouthful of his breakfast.

There was no other conversation for a few minutes as they ate. Kyle wiped his mouth with a napkin before looking at Brett.

"How long since you broke up with Louise?" he asked in his familiar Texas drawl.

"Eight months. It was the night of Jase's birthday," Brett replied with a nod at the other man.

"And how long were you together?" Kyle quizzed.

"Two years, give or take."

"And why did you break up?"

"What's with the twenty questions?" Brett retorted.

"Just curious. You weren't expecting Louise to end it, were you?" At Brett's shake of his head, Kyle continued. "You don't have to answer, but how were things between you before you broke up?"

"Well, obviously, they could have been better, otherwise I wouldn't be single now, would I?" Brett couldn't help replying sarcastically. Jase gave him a surprised look. It wasn't like him to snap at his friends.

"Sorry, Kyle. I know you mean well." He stared unseeing at his plate as he gathered his thoughts. "If I'm honest, I knew things weren't great between us, those last few months. We hardly saw each other, and when we did, I could sense she wanted more but I couldn't find it in me to give it."

Charlie gave him an encouraging nod as he asked, "What do you mean?"

"I knew she wanted to get married, but even though I loved her, I felt like something was missing, but I didn't know what it was. Still don't, actually."

"What was your sex life like?" Stuart asked.

"Why does it always come down to sex with you?"

"It doesn't always come down to sex with me," Stuart shot back. "I'm serious. Was it earth-shaking, can't keep your hands off each other, burn up the sheets sex? Or was it, insert tab A into slot B and go with the flow sex?"

Brett gaped at his best friend. "I…um…wow. I'm not sure how to answer that."

"Why not? It's a simple question with a simple answer."

"Does the first one even exist? Or is it a product of those romance novels I know you read on the sly?"

Muffled laughter met Brett's response, and he turned to the others.

"Oh, mate. Yes, the first one *definitely* exists," Charlie said with a wicked grin.

"Says the man whose boyfriend is the hottest rock star in the world," Brett pointed out. Charlie shrugged and took a drink from his coffee mug.

"He's right. It's only out of respect for Stu that we *didn't* defile his shower, or his spare bed this morning," Jase said, grinning at them.

"Like that's stopped you in the past," Stu said with a laugh.

"True, but enough about our sex lives. Brett, you've obviously been missing out," Jase said.

"Or been doing it wrong," Stu chimed in.

"Hang on. I've not had any complaints. I know how to have sex."

"I should hope so. But there are many levels of sex. You've just admitted to not having the earth-shaking kind, so maybe that something you felt was missing with Lou was the level of attraction, resulting in just okay sex," Stuart said matter-of-factly.

Brett glared at his oldest friend. "Of course I was attracted to Louise. She's beautiful."

"How long were you with Lou before you slept with her?" Kyle's expression was thoughtful.

"And when was the last time you slept together before she broke it off?" Stu added.

Brett pushed away from the table. "Look, guys, thanks for the concern, but I don't need you dissecting my sex life."

"Sorry, mate. We're only trying to help," Charlie said gently, ever the peacemaker.

"I appreciate it. I really do, but just because you lot are all loved up"—he glanced at Stu—"well, except for you, doesn't mean everyone around you has to be."

"I may not be loved up like these three saps, but I'm getting plenty of lovin'," Stu said with a smirk. "You know what they say: 'if you can't be with the one you love, love the one you're with.'"

"One- or two-night stands are not love. Even *I* know that." Brett gave his friend a gentle shove on the shoulder. "When *you* find that one person to settle down with, then I will let you organise my love life."

Stu laughed. "Like that will ever happen. Settling down with one person long term is not in my DNA. I'll leave that to you guys."

"Famous last words, my friend," Charlie said to him. He glanced at Jase and Kyle. "How much do you want to bet he falls in love in the next year?"

Brett laughed at the glare Stu was giving Charlie. "See, it's not so much fun when it's your love life, is it?"

"At least I have a love life," Stu told him pointedly.

"Okay. I admit it. The sex may not have been earth shattering, but it wasn't bad."

"And by not bad you mean you got off," Stu said with a raised eyebrow.

"Well, I made sure she did too," Brett replied, a blush staining his cheeks. He was a little uncomfortable having his lack of sex life dissected by his friends. He should have been used to the candid talk, he'd never known them to be shy about talking about their own, and after so many years of knowing them, it was just part of the norm, even if he wasn't as forthcoming as they were.

"I'm sure you are a very generous lover, B, but there's getting off and then there's getting off so hard you can't remember your name."

"Really? Sure it's not just something else that happens in those books you read?"

A deep sigh came from across the table, and Brett looked at Jase, who was giving his boyfriend such a heated look that Brett's skin prickled.

"Hey, you two. Less of the eye-fucking at the table please," Charlie said with a laugh. "Some of us have to wait another three weeks before we can do that!"

"And some of us only have to wait until tonight," Stu said from the kitchen where he was cleaning up.

"You going out on the town tonight?" Charlie asked.

"Yeah. Wanna come with?" Stuart sat back down at the table with a fresh mug of coffee and eyed his best friend. "In fact, why don't you come with me, B. I'm sure we can get you hooked up."

Brett shook his head. "Thanks for the offer, but besides the fact I'm on early shift in the morning, I doubt there'll be anyone at the bars you're going to that will catch my eye."

"Maybe that's what's missing?" Stuart mused, mischief shining in his blue eyes.

"What do you mean?" Brett frowned at his friend.

"Maybe the reason you feel you're missing something is because you are. Maybe you need to come over to our side of the fence and dip your…toe in the big gay pond."

"Guys, you know I love each one of you. I'm proud to call you my closest and best friends, but after knowing you for so many years, don't you think I would have figured out I was attracted to men by now?"

"Maybe you haven't met the right guy yet?" Stuart countered.

"I'm thirty-one. I've been looking at girls since I was twelve years old. I'm sure."

"Yes, but surely you've met a guy and thought he's attractive?" Stuart pushed.

"Well, of course he has. He's met all of us," Charlie said with a laugh, gesturing to the table. "And I won't even get jealous when you admit that my boyfriend is the hottest guy you've ever met."

The table erupted in laughter. Brett shook his head at his friends. "True, you guys are all good looking. And, duh, your boyfriend is Cooper-freaking-Evans. I'm not blind, just not attracted to you all. Thank God."

"Hey, what's wrong with us?" Jase protested with a mock pout.

Kyle leaned over and kissed his Jase on the cheek. "You're perfect, darlin'. And as much as I am enjoying this conversation, we need to get a move on if we're going to get to the open home in time."

"True. Thanks for the bed-and-breakfast, Stu." Jase stood up from the table.

"Open home? You guys buying a place?" Charlie asked.

The couple swapped a glance before Jase replied, "Yeah. My place is fine, but we want something a little bigger for when Kyle's family come to visit."

"That's great news. Let us know how it goes," Brett congratulated them as he stood to leave as well. "I'll get moving too."

"What are you doing today?" Stuart asked him.

"I'll hit the gym and then home to prep for work. Tonight, I'll just chill, watch the game."

"If you change your mind, give me a yell. Y'know you're always welcome to come and hang out," Stuart said.

Brett picked up his keys and phone from where he'd left them the night before. "I'd hate to cramp your style, mate." He turned as he got to the door. "Just remember, I'm on at seven in the morning, so if you need to send out the bat signal, it needs to be before then."

"I haven't had to use that in months," Stu said with a laugh.

"Have a good night. I'll catch you all later," Brett called out as he left the house.

Two hours later he was pulling into the driveway of the large four-bedroom house he shared with three others. His flatmates were a few years younger than him, but they all got on okay. It wasn't Brett's ideal situation, but after he and Louise had broken up, he'd had to give up the small unit they had shared as her parents owned it.

He noticed there were several cars parked on the street in front of the house, and he gave an internal sigh. It looked like they had company. He hoped it wasn't for the night as he liked to have a quiet one before he started his four-day shift rotation.

Letting himself in, he could hear raised voices coming from the kitchen at the rear of the house. He dropped his gym bag in his room before going to investigate. Rounding the corner, it surprised him to see the property manager and the landlord there with his flatmates.

"Ah, Mr Parker, there you are. I was just about to ring you," the property manager greeted him.

"What's going on? Why are you both here? Did we have an inspection today I wasn't told about?" he asked, looking at his flatmates.

Doug, a tall redhead, shook his head. Before he could answer though, the property manager spoke again.

"When we did the property inspection last month, you mentioned there had been problems with the drainage in the back garden."

Brett nodded his agreement. "Yeah. It's been smelling too, especially after all the rain we've had recently."

"It turns out that the main storm water drain and the sewage pipes have partially collapsed, which means the whole yard will have to be dug up and the pipes re-laid."

"That will be a big job," Brett said, turning to look at their landlord.

"Yes, it is. Unfortunately, it means I can't allow you to stay here while the work is being done. It's a health and safety issue," Mr Wong said with a shrug.

"It means we have to move out, Brett. Like, in the next couple of weeks," Doug told him.

"What? How long for?" Brett asked, a sinking feeling coming over him. He hated moving, and trying to find a new place would be hard. Not many people enjoyed flatting with a shift worker.

"Once the work is complete, I'll put the property on the market. It is getting too expensive for me to keep doing maintenance."

"So, basically you're evicting us," Brett told him, keeping a hold on his rising frustration.

"My hands are tied. You can't be here when the work is being done. I'm sorry, Mr Parker. You are good tenants. I will give you all a good reference, but you need to be out in two weeks' time."

"And because of the short notice, Mr Wong has agreed to waive your rent for the rest of your lease," the property manager added with a kind smile.

"Well, I suppose that's something." Brett blew out a sigh. "I'm on shift for the next four days, so if there's anything else, can you email or text me? I'll get back to you when I can."

"Of course," Mr Wong nodded.

The property manager and landlord left a few minutes later, leaving Brett with Doug and their other flatmates, Henri and Natalie.

"Are we going to find another place that will take all four of us?" Doug asked.

"I'm good with that, if you guys want to." Brett nodded.

Henri and Natalie shared a look before Natalie spoke. "Um. We were planning to tell you in the next couple of weeks, but I've been offered a job in Wellington, and Henri is coming with me."

"I thought there was something going on with you two," Doug said with a grin.

"Huh. Well, I missed it," Brett said, looking between the two. "Congrats. I hope it all works out for you."

"Thanks, Brett," Natalie said. "You and Doug can still get a place together though."

"Yeah. I'll ask around. The guys at the station may know of somewhere."

After more discussion, the four parted ways, and Brett disappeared into his room. It frustrated him, and he didn't want to move but understood the reasons. After getting his work bag ready and making sure his uniform was prepared, he made himself a simple dinner of chicken and pasta with enough left over for his lunch the following day.

As he lay on his bed, the game playing on his small television, he thought back to his conversation that morning with the guys. What he'd told them wasn't completely true; he'd not just looked at women. Sometimes he'd seen a guy who had made him look twice, and once, he'd caught Jase and Kyle making out. He remembered thinking they looked hot together and wondering what it would be like to be with a guy.

He hadn't wanted to admit to the guys that his and Lou's sex life had been lacklustre in the last few months, both going through the motions. They'd never been adventurous, and now he thought about it, Lou had always let him do all the work. He could count on one hand the amount of times she'd initiated sex in the two years they'd been together, and her idea of foreplay had been a quick tug or two on his dick and then lying there while he made sure she was turned on and ready.

He'd asked her what she wanted and liked, hoping she'd take the hint and ask him the same, but she hadn't. More often than not, he'd ended up watching porn to get off when she wasn't there as it had been slightly more satisfying.

Thinking about sex, or the lack thereof, had him switching off his TV and reaching for his tablet. He brought up his favourite porn site and scanned through the scenes. He clicked on one and watched as the leggy brunette stripped for the guy holding the camera. His dick thickened, and he slipped his hand into his boxers and gave it a pull. A blond guy joined the girl on the bed, and they began by making out before the scene jumped and there were two guys with the girl.

As the three of them writhed together, Brett got harder. He stripped off his boxers and stroked himself. The blond was thrusting into the girl, who was letting out high-pitched moans and groans, when the second guy leaned over and kissed the other man before kneeling behind him and rubbing his hard cock into the seam of the blond's arse.

Brett became transfixed on the males rather than the woman, his hand moving faster on his own cock. He was close to coming when the scene cut off and then ended. Groaning, he kept stroking himself, but it wasn't enough. He tried picturing himself thrusting into the leggy brunette, but all he could see behind his closed eyes was the two guys rubbing together.

He let go of himself and did a quick search on the website for two men. He watched a couple frotting together, their deeper moans and harsh grunts making him harder, and his strokes became faster and firmer. As the men on camera came, his own release barrelled through him, leaving him panting as he slowed his hand and gentled his grip.

He lay for a few minutes before switching off his tablet and cleaning himself up with some tissues. As he settled under the covers, the familiar hollow settled over him as the post-orgasmic glow wore off. It wasn't the first time he'd watched gay porn, and he didn't want to examine too closely why he found it more of a turn on than heterosexual porn. He didn't want to admit that maybe he wasn't as straight as everyone thought.

Chapter Two

Brett pulled into the staff parking area behind the squat, brick fire station He grabbed his bag from the back seat and quickly jogged through the light drizzle to the warm building. After storing his gear in his locker, he made his way into the brightly lit kitchen area and put his lunch into the fridge. His shift didn't officially start until eight, but as was tradition, his team arrived an hour before to allow the night shift crew time to hand over before they headed home.

"How was your night?" Brett asked the overnight shift commander while making a coffee.

"Pretty quiet, thank goodness," Pete replied, chuckling. "Looks like we got more sleep than you did."

Brett ran a hand over his face. "I had a quiet one but had a crap night's sleep."

"Something on your mind?"

"Landlord needs us to move out and just one of those nights when you wake up more tired than when you went to bed," Brett replied, not wanting to explain the dreams he'd had all night. Dreams of naked men. He'd woken half-hard and confused. He'd decided that watching male-on-male porn before going to sleep was not something he should make a regular habit of.

"Hopefully you guys will have an uneventful shift too," Pete told him as the rest of Brett's Watch began to filter into the room.

"You've probably jinxed us now with that comment. Thanks, mate!" Brett replied with a laugh before greeting the other members of his team.

"Hey, Chalky, saw a bloke that just looked like you at the Smoking Keg on Friday night," Ray, Brett's teammate, called out to the newest member of the group.

"Probably was me," Paul 'Chalky' White replied. "What time were you there?"

"Nah, can't have been you. This bloke was wrapped around another guy, getting very up close and personal."

A knowing grin spread across the younger man's face. "Oh, yeah. Definitely was me then."

"But you're straight, aren't you?" Ray spluttered. "You introduced us to that girl you were seeing at Easter."

"I'm bi," Chalky said with a shrug.

"You are?" Ray wrinkled his brow in confusion.

"Is that a problem?" Brett asked before Chalky could respond.

"Nah, course not," Ray rushed to reassure Chalky and Brett. "What he does out of work is no concern of mine."

The station officer, Les, interrupted them. "Okay, you lot. Enough chin wag. Let's get this show on the road so Green Watch can bugger off home."

After roll call, Brett was allocated to equipment check with Chalky. His teammate had only been in the fire service since the beginning of the year but had taken to the job like a seasoned professional.

"Thanks for saying something earlier," Chalky said, "but you didn't have to."

"I know I didn't, but some of the older guys are a bit set in their ways."

"So you're okay with it?" Chalky asked as he put the first aid kit back into the cab of the engine they were checking.

Brett laughed. "Mate, most of my friends are gay. I have no problem whatsoever with anyone's sexuality."

"Really? Most of your friends are gay?" Chalky looked at him in surprise. At Brett's nod, he gave a short laugh. "So, you're what…? Bi? Gay? Pan?"

"Straight."

"Really?" Chalky asked again. "You've never been curious? With all your friends being gay, you must have been tempted?"

Memories of last night's dreams flashed through Brett's mind and he prayed he wasn't blushing. He gave Chalky a big grin. "Attracted to those ugly bastards? Nah, mate." He brushed off the suggestion, hoping Chalky believed him. He didn't want to dwell on last night.

Chalky seemed to accept his statement, and they continued to work through the maintenance checklist. Curiosity got the better of Brett though.

"So have you always known you're bi?" he asked casually.

"Pretty much. When I was a hormonal teen, I was popping wood all the time, regardless of whether it was a hot girl or a hot guy." Chalky grinned at Brett. "I did a little experimenting and talked to the counsellors at school. Once I understood that it was okay to be attracted to both sexes, well, let's just say, I've never been lonely."

"And your family are okay with it?"

"They are now. Was hard for them to understand at first how I could be out with a girl one weekend and then bringing a guy home for dinner the next. They came around eventually though, and as long as I'm happy, they're happy."

"How'd you end up with a group of gay friends?" Chalky asked him as they finished up and headed towards the kitchen for a coffee break.

"It started out with my best friend from school coming out when we were thirteen. And when he went off to uni, he made friends with a couple of other gay guys, and now they're the people I mainly hang out with."

"Ah, I see. You're the token straight friend," Chalky teased, dodging out of the way as Brett cuffed him over the shoulder.

"No. There are other straight friends in the group. It's never been a thing. We hang out 'cos we like each other. Who each of us sleeps with is not an issue."

"So, are any of these friends single?" Chalky asked with a quirk of his eyebrow, his eyes glittering with mischief.

"A year ago, I would have said yes, but now, only one is, and he's happy to be that way."

"That's a shame." Chalky was interrupted from saying anything more as the alarm sounded and the slightly robotic voice of the comms dispatcher echoed through the station. Both men put their coffee mugs into the sink before jumping into the engine, their conversation forgotten.

Eight hours later, Brett was once again pulling into the driveway at home. Thankfully, Pete hadn't jinxed them, and their day had been fairly uneventful, with only the one call out to a rubbish bin fire at the local park.

His flatmates were all home, slouched in the lounge watching a movie. After calling out a greeting to them, Brett headed for a shower before fixing himself something to eat. As he pottered in the kitchen, Doug appeared to grab a beer from the fridge.

"Did you have time to ask the guys at work about a flat?" Doug asked him as he leaned against the counter.

"I mentioned it, but no one knows of anything. You had any luck?"

Doug gave him a sheepish look. "My sister-in-law's brother has a room going and it's close to work."

Brett sighed and smiled wanly at Doug. "Go for it, mate. I'll find somewhere, don't worry."

"Sorry, Brett. I asked if there was room for two, but there's not."

"It's fine. Don't worry. I'll message my mates. I'm sure they'll know of something." Brett took his dinner and headed to his room. He didn't feel like company tonight.

As he ate, he opened the group message chat he had with the guys.

Brett: *Hey—about to be homeless. Know of any rooms or flats going?*

A few minutes later, his phone pinged.

Charlie: *Homeless? Who'd you piss off now?*

Brett: *No one. Landlord's kicking us all out. Got two weeks to find a place.*

Charlie: *You know you can stay here any time.*

Brett: *Thanks but it's too far out. Maybe if I get desperate*

Jase: *My place will be empty soon, but not in two weeks, sorry.*

Stu: *Move in here.*

Brett: *?*

Stu: *You can stay here until you get a place. You can put your shit in the garage.*

Brett: *You sure? I wouldn't want to cramp your style.*

Stu: *Ha ha*

Brett: *Thanks mate. I'll call you tomorrow night after work.*

Stu: *Come for dinner.*

Brett: *Ok. See you later.*

He lay in bed, struggling to read his book, but his mind kept replaying the conversation with Chalky, and the dreams he'd had the night before. He'd never really considered his friends as anything but friends. Sure, he could acknowledge they were good looking, but he'd not looked at them sexually. Never really thought about what they did in the privacy of their own homes, just as he presumed they never worried about what he and Louise used to do.

He gave up trying to read and willed himself to relax and sleep. After last night's vivid dreams, he wasn't going to look at any more videos of either straight or gay porn before sleeping.

Chapter Three

The squeak of the marker against the whiteboard was drowned out by the muffled giggles of the class of sixteen- and seventeen-year-olds. With his back to them, Stuart pretended to ponder what he was going to write next as he fought to stop himself from joining in the stifled mirth. Schooling his face into a semi-serious expression, he put the cap on the pen and turned around. He deliberately let his gaze wander over them, noting which of them had a sudden interest in the desk in front of them, trying to avoid his eyes.

He tapped the marker against his chin as he perched his hip on the edge of his desk, focusing on the slouched boy in the back row. "Mr Lewis, would you like to tell me why I can hear laughing?"

"Because you have ears…sir?" came the snorted reply as the rest of the class dissolved into laughter.

Stuart rolled his eyes before joining them. "Alright, smart-arse, that's enough of that." He stood up from his desk and returned to the whiteboard. "Are there any other key moments from *Captain America* that you think we have missed?"

There were murmurs from the group but no further ideas. "Okay then, your homework is to pick one of these things we have listed and start your personal response to it."

There were a couple of groans, the loudest from Jack Lewis. "Problem, Jack?" Stuart asked.

"Do we have to, sir? I mean, what use is this going to be when I'm fixing cars?"

"Probably not a great deal in a practical sense, but bosses like workers who can interact intelligently with their customers and work mates. Being able to string a sentence together and have a valid discussion about something, whether it be the latest blockbuster movie or a new technical innovation in the motor industry, is a skill that you will need. This exercise helps you develop that."

"Mr Johnson?" another student called out.

"Yes, Sam?" Stuart smiled at one of the quiet achievers in the class.

"Is it really fair to expect Jack to do anything intelligently?" he asked before grinning at his best friend.

"Oy, you little shi…" Jack's outraged cry was suddenly cut off by the ringing of the fire alarm. Chairs scraped across the floor as the students jumped to their feet, frantically trying to push their books into their bags.

"Okay, guys, calm down. It's probably just a drill. Grab your gear and make your way onto the field to the assembly point," Stuart called out to them as he reached into his desk drawer for his wallet, keys, and phone. They weren't supposed to take personal items with them, but he didn't like leaving them behind.

"Sir, I don't think it's a drill. I think something's happened in the science lab," one of the girls, Lyndsey, said, pointing to the adjoining block where students were coming out with panicked looks on their faces.

"Keep moving, you lot. Walk, don't run, and head straight to your tutor group." Stuart ushered them out before pulling the classroom door closed behind him. He turned and headed against the stream of teenagers.

Reaching the science block, he saw his colleague coughing as he urged the last of the students out. "Reg, are you okay?" he asked the older man.

Reg wheezed out a cough. "I'll be fine. Just a little smoke inhalation. One of the kids knocked over a Bunsen burner and it caught onto his notebook. I managed to put it out, but of course the detectors went off."

Stu quickly stuck his head in the classroom to make sure it was clear before closing the door and taking Reg by the arm. The man was close to retiring age and had recently been out sick with the flu. He was looking decidedly pale and coughs were wracking his body.

"Come on. Let's get you out of here." He gently led Reg out of the building, hearing the sirens of the approaching fire service. He knew they would be here quickly as the station was only a few hundred metres up the road.

He handed Reg off to the school nurse, who had hurried over with the first aid kit, before joining other staff members in trying to keep nearly two thousand teenagers corralled. Stu hoped the fire service guys wouldn't take too long before giving the all clear. He'd not thought to grab his jacket, and although the sun was out, it was the tail end of winter and there was a stiff breeze blowing across the open playing fields.

Twenty minutes later the officer in charge was happy there was no further danger and the ringing bell of the fire alarm was shut off. With a sigh of relief, he started herding the kids back towards the classrooms. His class had officially ended ten minutes ago, so he decided to grab a coffee from the staff room before heading to his room to tidy up and start on the grading he had to do.

"Hey, Stu!"

He grinned at the sight of his best friend jogging towards him. He took a second to admire the way Brett looked in his turnout gear. Although the bulky jacket and pants did nothing to show off Brett's athletic body, there was something about it that always made Stu look twice when he saw Brett kitted out for work.

"Hey, mate. Wondered if you were about," he said with a grin.

Brett took off his helmet and brushed back his dark blond hair. "Yeah, few more hours to go. Glad this wasn't too bad. Got a bit worried when I heard we were coming here."

"It was only a minor incident, thank goodness. You still up for dinner tonight?

"Yes, if the offer's still open?"

"Course it is," Stuart confirmed. He noticed Lyndsey from his class dawdling with her best friend, casting glances towards him and Brett. "Come on, girls, get a move on," he called out to them, waving a hand at them to hurry up.

"I'll leave you to it," Brett said with a grin.

"See you later."

With a wave, Brett jogged back towards the fire appliance. Stuart's gaze lingered on his retreating form. *Yep, looked as good from the back.*

"Mr Johnson?" Stuart turned to find Lyndsey and her friend staring at him.

"Yes, Lyndsay?"

"Is that cute fireman your boyfriend?" she asked, blushing slightly as her friend giggled next to her.

"Who? Brett?" Stuart laughed. "No. He's just my best friend."

"So, is he single then, sir?" she asked with a sly grin.

"Firstly, he is nearly twice your age, so you can get *that* thought of your head. And secondly, you are supposed to be in class. Now scoot." He pointed towards the classroom block.

The girls gave a final giggle before walking slightly faster off the field.

Stuart grinned internally. He must remember to tell Brett that the girls thought he was his boyfriend. It wouldn't be the first time someone had asked the same thing, and at one time he'd wanted it to be true. He and Brett had been friends since they were eleven years old.

Though they had both gone to different high schools after the two years at Intermediate school, their friendship had grown and solidified as they played on the same soccer teams through their teens.

Stuart didn't publicise his sexuality, but he didn't hide the fact he was gay either. If a student asked, he was honest with them, and he sat on the school LGBTQ committee that ran events and offered a safe environment for those students who needed it. He was pleased there was more acceptance now than when he had been in high school, but there was still a long way to go.

Two hours later the final bell of the day sounded, and Stuart closed down his laptop and packed up his gear. He trudged to his car, dodging the usual madness of students streaming out into the watery afternoon sun as they rushed to catch buses or get to after-school activities. The day had been long, and he was so ready to be home.

A familiar sense of peace enveloped him as he let himself into his small three-bedroom house. He quickly changed out of his work clothes and headed to the kitchen to rustle up a snack.

As he rummaged in the pantry, Bucky wound his way around Stuart's feet, and he reached down to pick up the purring feline.

"Hey, Bucky. How was your day?" he asked, giving him a scratch under the chin. Bucky's ears flicked, and he gave a wriggle, and Stuart let him down. "Where's your brother?" Bucky replied with a plaintive yowl and nudged at Stu's leg.

With a grin, Stu reached into the pantry for a tin of cat food. As soon as he pulled on the ring tab to open it, the pet door in the laundry room clattered and a pale ginger streak shot into the kitchen.

Stuart chuckled as he spooned food into the waiting bowls. "There you are, Cap. Glad to see your hearing is as good as ever." The large tomcat gave a loud mewl as he nudged Stuarts's ankle. "Alright, alright, hang on a minute."

He placed the bowls down, and both cats set on them hungrily. Leaving his obviously undernourished animals to eat, he took his snack to his favourite chair in the lounge.

He was engrossed in a book when his phone chirped, the pre-set reminder going off. With a sigh, he flipped the cover to his Kindle closed, putting the device to sleep. He'd got to a really tense part in the story and wanted to see how it played out. The author was notorious for plot twists and keeping the reader guessing. But he'd have to wait. Brett was due to arrive soon and dinner wouldn't cook itself.

He had nearly finished prepping the food when he heard Brett's car pull into the driveway. A single knock sounded at the door as it was opened, and Brett called out his name.

"Kitchen," he called back.

Brett wandered in, similarly dressed in loose sweats and an old soccer club hoodie, carrying a six pack of beer, which he placed on the island bench along with his keys and phone.

"Hey, mate. How'd your day finish up?" Brett asked as he opened one of the beers and passed it to Stu.

"It was my last class of the day, so I marked some papers and then came home. How 'bout you?"

"Nothing after your call out." Brett peered at the ingredients laid out on the bench. "What are we having?"

"Chorizo and roast veg salad," Stu replied as he began to prepare their meal. They chatted as he worked, finally getting around to the topic of Brett moving in.

"Are you sure you want me here? I meant it when I said I didn't want to cramp your style," Brett told him as they sat down to eat.

"You're my best mate, of course I don't mind. How many times did I stay at yours when we were growing up? You can move in this week if you like. Your big stuff will be fine in the garage and you can just use the furniture in the spare room."

"Thanks, I really appreciate it. I go onto nights tomorrow, so I'll start packing up and then move my gear over on Thursday after I wake up, if that suits."

"That'll be good. Give Charlie a buzz and see if he's free and if we can use his ute to move your bed over."

They finalised details as they finished off their meal and, after cleaning up, settled onto the couch to catch the sports highlights from the weekend.

"So, how'd you go on Saturday night? Did you find someone to bring home?" Brett teased.

"Nah. Had a few drinks and a couple of dances." Stuart shrugged.

"Don't tell me you're getting picky in your old age?"

"Yeah, nah. No one caught my fancy, and, contrary to popular belief, I am actually a bit choosy about who I shag these days."

"Whatever, mate. I believe ya; thousands wouldn't," Brett said with a wink.

"Don't give me that. You're worse than I am. At least I'm going out and looking. You rarely do," Stu shot back. "Hey, you'll be off Saturday night, won't you?"

"Yeah, I'm off Thursday to Sunday this week." Brett eyed his friend suspiciously. "Why?"

"You and me. We're going out Saturday night."

"Why, Stuart. Are you asking me on a date?" He grinned at his best friend.

Stu rolled his eyes. "You wish. Besides, you know I don't date."

"I don't get why you don't want to settle down. Any guy would be lucky to have you as his partner, Stu. You've got a lot to offer."

"Pfff. Like I had great role models growing up on what a loving relationship should be. I'd be a crap boyfriend, and you know it. I'm too set in my ways, just like my parents are. I like my space and I'm happy with my own company. Having to come home and make nice with someone when all I want to do is curl up with a book and they want to chat or go out or have people over. Ugh. No thanks. I'll stick to my hook-ups and my cats, thank you very much."

"You're going to end up a lonely and grumpy old man if you're not careful," Brett warned him as he stood up to leave.

"Whatever." Stu dismissed the conversation with a wave of his hand. "Just start bringing your stuff over when you like. I'll make sure the wardrobe and drawers are empty."

"Thanks. I really appreciate you helping me out here. Hopefully it won't be for long and you can get back to being a grumpy old cat-man."

Stuart gave him the finger as he waved him off but it was a show of false bravado.

Brett's words had stung a little, and he rubbed his chest absently, willing away the hurt he'd felt. Not everyone was made for a relationship, and there was nothing wrong with how he lived his life. He wished his friends would just let him be. Just because they were all coupled up and in love didn't mean he had to be. He knew they only had his best interests at heart, but it didn't stop the frustration he felt when they started in on him about how he lived his life.

Chapter Four

Brett woke with a start, heart racing and a fine layer of sweat on his skin. He bolted upright, his brain struggling to catch up with his consciousness. He glanced around the dimly lit room, trying to figure out where he was. All at once the dots connected, and he recognised the semi familiar layout of Stuart's spare bedroom—now his—and that he had been dreaming.

He eased back onto the pillow and took a deep breath to steady himself, closing his eyes. His subconscious flashed pictures from the vivid dream he'd been having. He gasped as memories of tangled limbs, mouths meeting, and groans and moans echoed through his brain. His dick was semi-hard. A vision of rubbing against another man popped into his mind, and his hips gave an involuntary jerk. *What the fuck?*

As he tried to make sense of why he was turned on and why he'd been dreaming of making out with a guy, he heard a long, low moan followed by a muffled curse. Brett's eyes snapped open as a second groan echoed through the house and then a recognisable rhythmic bump coming from the adjacent room. Brett gave his own internal groan and grabbed the spare pillow and put it over his head.

As promised, Stuart had dragged him out to their favourite haunt, The Smoking Keg. They'd had a few drinks, and Brett had danced with a couple of girls but really hadn't been into the whole night at all. He'd lost sight of Stu and had messaged him to say he was heading home. A thumbs-up emoji had been his only reply, and he'd figured, obviously correctly, that Stu had found company.

The pillow over his head didn't block out the shouts of "*Oh, yes. Fuck yes. Fuck yes.*" Rolling over onto his stomach, he pulled both pillows over his head to try to dull the noise, but it was a wasted effort. Stu's companion was very vocal and very loud. Brett stretched across the mattress and tried to remember where the earbuds for his phone were. He'd plug into his favourite playlist and hopefully that would work. Shuffling to reach into the bedside drawer, his semi-hard cock dragged against the sheet, and he unconsciously rolled his hips.

He pulled the drawer open and reached in blindly, feeling for the wires, but got side-tracked as he rocked back and forth, pushing down to increase the friction on his hardening erection. The sounds from the other room were gaining in momentum, and Brett found himself moving in time. Closing his eyes, images from his dream flashed behind his eyelids, causing him to moan and roll over to reach his leaking dick. He stroked himself, spreading pre-come down his shaft as he reached with his other hand to fondle his balls before pressing against the taut skin below them.

"Oh yes. I'm there. Harder. Don't stop." The cries from Stu's room spurred Brett on, his hand stroking in time to the thump of the bed against the wall. Throwing his other arm above his head, he gripped at the slats in the headboard and stretched his body taut. He imagined a hot mouth travelling down his body, sucking and nipping at his skin. He held back a whimper as he drew his knees up and dug his heels into the bed, hand moving faster as the familiar heat of his orgasm built in his groin. He heard the low timbre of Stu's voice encouraging his lover and for a brief second, Brett imagined it was him Stu was fucking. With that thought, along with a quick tweak to his nipples, Brett came spurting onto his belly and chest. He barely registered the long drawn-out shout from next door as he rode out the waves coursing through his body.

Brett's breath came in short pants as he returned to reality. He could hear murmurs through the wall, and mortification rolled through him as the realisation he'd got off to hearing his best friend having sex set in. He eased off the bed, about to go and clean up, when he heard the door to Stu's room open. He froze. He didn't want Stu to know what he'd just done. It was going to be hard enough to look the man in the eye in the morning. Deciding to stay where he was, he pulled a t-shirt from his dirty laundry hamper and wiped himself down.

He crept under the sheets and tried not to listen for any further noises coming from next door. He willed himself back to sleep, praying he wouldn't be woken up again.

Sunlight filtered around the edges of the heavy curtains when Brett woke later. He stretched and let out a contented sigh, feeling well rested. The toot of a car horn and movement in the hallway outside his room had memories of the night before flooding back, and his relaxed vibe disappeared instantly. Guilt and shame warred with embarrassment, and he scrubbed his face with his hands as his stomach gave a slow, nauseating roll. He took a deep breath to try to settle his stomach and clear his mind. *It was nothing.* He'd gotten off to porn; how was this any different? *Because it was your best friend, idiot,* his subconscious screamed at back him. Cursing his traitorous mind and body, he willed himself to stay calm. He just needed to carry on as if nothing had happened. Stu would never know, and Brett would make sure his earbuds were closer to hand in the future.

The sound of the bathroom door closing had him jumping out of bed. Pulling on an old pair of sweats and a clean t-shirt, he left his room and headed for the kitchen to make coffee before Stu appeared. It would give him a few more valuable minutes to relax and keep everything normal.

Stu had two coffee machines: a pod machine and a fancier barista type. Brett didn't mind the pod coffee but preferred a more traditional espresso and set about preparing a cup. As he heard the bathroom door open, he called out to his friend.

"Do you want a coffee? I'm making the real stuff."

"Please," came the muffled reply.

Good. This was good. Normal routine. Nothing to see here, Brett thought to himself as he reached for a mug to make a second drink.

Stu wandered into the kitchen moments later, his movements slow and heavy, barely acknowledging his friend as he made his way to the fridge. Brett smirked at the sight. Stu was always better once he'd had a strong dose of caffeine and food after a night out.

With one hand covering a yawn, Stu passed the milk to Brett before pulling out a bottle of fresh orange juice. Brett nodded his thanks, not commenting as Stu poured himself a glass before reaching into the cupboard above the counter and getting out a small pill container. He shook one out and swallowed it down with a grimace.

"Why are you taking a little blue pill at this time of the morning, when your date has just left?" Brett asked him with a grin, breaking the silence.

Stuart rinsed out the glass before placing it next to the sink. "Ha ha. It's not a pill to get me going; it's a tablet to keep me safe," Stu retorted, his voice husky with sleep.

"Mate, hate to tell you, but you can't get pregnant, so the morning-after pill is a bit of a waste of time." Leaning against the counter, he laughed as his friend rolled his eyes at him.

"It's PrEP," Stu told him before taking a mouthful of his coffee, eyes closing, a look of bliss crossing his features.

"Prepping you for what? Is it a long action thing that you take hours before you need it?"

Blue eyes popped open. "Seriously? You've never heard of Truvada?"

Brett shook his head. "Nope. Is it like a cousin to Viagra?"

"Truvada is a pre-exposure prophylaxis. I take one every day to reduce the risk of becoming infected with HIV."

"What? Is that a possibility? I thought you were careful," Brett said as he eyed his friend up and down, searching for signs of what, he didn't know.

"Of course it's a possibility and of course I'm always careful," Stu reassured him, "but accidents with condoms can happen, and giving a blow-job to a guy wearing a condom isn't my favourite thing. And don't get me started on flavoured condoms, they're one of the most disgusting inventions ever thought of."

Brett gaped at his friend. "You're okay though? You're not sick or anything?"

"I had a close call earlier this year, when I got home from Sydney." Stu sighed, obviously not happy about explaining. "I'm tested every three months, and it was a false positive result. I had another test done straight away, and it came back negative. The doc and I decided to be on the safe side, so now I take a pill every day to help protect me. It's not one hundred percent certain, but it's better than doing nothing."

"How come you never said anything at the time? You know I would have been there for you," Brett told him, hurt fuelled by worry and fear racing through him. He didn't like the idea that his friend had faced a huge health scare on his own. *Damn him for his independence and I-don't-need-anyone attitude.*

Stu shrugged nonchalantly. "Really, it was no big deal. There wasn't anything you could do, and it all turned out fine in the end, so no harm done."

"Still. I'm your best mate, you should have said something. You're allowed to ask for help, you know. You don't have to do everything on your own." Brett huffed as he rinsed out his coffee mug. "What are your plans today?" he asked, changing the subject before his annoyance got the better of him and he said something stupid.

"Sleep. Netflix. A book. Basically, fuck all," Stu replied. "Why, what are you up to?"

"Pretty much the same. Do my laundry and organise my food for the next few days of shift, so I need to do a grocery run at some point."

"Unless there's something special you want, just use what's in the freezer or pantry," Stu told him with a wave of his hand. "You can do groceries next week and replace what you use."

Brett nodded. He really didn't fancy tackling the supermarket that day. He chuckled as Stu gave another huge yawn. "Go back to bed. From the sounds of it, you didn't get much rest last night."

Stu winked at him, features brightening in amusement. "You're right, I didn't." He pushed away from the kitchen bench but paused as a thought obviously occurred to him. "Wait. Did you hear us?"

Brett cheeks warmed as he blushed. "Ah, yeah, your partner sounded very enthusiastic?" He cringed internally at the way his voice rose slightly, making the statement into a question.

"Oh, he was. Sorry, mate. Didn't mean to wake you. We didn't keep you up though, did we?" Stu's eyes twinkled with mirth as he took in Brett's embarrassment.

"What? No. Course not. I…um…barely heard you. Just rolled over and went back to sleep." Brett rubbed a hand through his hair. "I'm going to go and have a shower. I'll catch you later."

Brett hurried out of the kitchen. He'd managed to act normally all morning, but now he felt awkward. He didn't want Stu to think he was a perv, getting off on hearing two guys having sex. He pushed the thoughts away and focussed on his plans for the rest of the day.

*****

Stu watched with amusement as Brett disappeared up the hallway. His friend obviously felt embarrassed hearing him and the guy he'd brought home from the club. Stu wasn't feeling any such embarrassment. It was only after Joey—*Johnny?*—had yelled out as he climaxed, that he had remembered Brett in the other room. That was one of the reasons he lived alone and didn't have a flatmate. He liked not having to worry if he or his partner were a bit vocal or loud. In fact, it was lucky that he and Joey—*yes, definitely Joey*—had made it to the bedroom. There weren't many places in the house that he hadn't had sex in or on.

He decided to make himself some breakfast before quickly going over his lesson plans for the week, then he could crash out for the rest of the day. Thank God it was the last week of term. He was looking forward to the two-week spring break before heading into the mad rush of the last term of the year. It was always chaotic with end-of-year exams, internal assessments, and the kids getting antsy as the weather warmed up and everyone, teachers included, counted down to the summer break over Christmas.

Brett wandered back into the room a while later and flopped down in the recliner. "What are you doing for your birthday next weekend?"

"Ugh, don't remind me," Stu replied, closing his laptop down.

"Why? You usually love your birthday. And it falls on Saturday, so we can head out and hit the town if you want. I'll rustle the guys up."

"I know, it's just that, well, now I'm officially in my thirties, y'know," Stu said.

"Mate, you've been in your thirties for a year. You're only turning thirty-one, not thirty-five. Really, it's not that bad." Brett laughed at him.

"True. To answer your question, I'm doing end-of-term drinks with some of the guys from work on Friday night and then my darling parents are gracing me with their presence and taking me out for lunch on Saturday."

Brett looked at him in surprise. "You mean, they're in the country this year and coming to see you on your actual birthday?"

"Yep," Stu said with a resigned sigh. "Edward and Beverly will be in Auckland for their only child's birthday."

"Wow. Did your dad forget to schedule a speaking engagement somewhere?"

Stu huffed out a laugh. "Oh, no, Dr Johnson is speaking at the University of Auckland on Friday before he and my mother dine with the local academia bigwigs. They have just enough time to squeeze in lunch with their son before they head back to Wellington on the afternoon flight."

"Okay, so Saturday night will definitely require alcohol in large amounts to nullify the parent effect. Don't worry about a thing; I'll make sure we have a night to remember."

"Sounds good," Stuart said before stretching. "Chuck us the remote, there must be a movie on or something I can watch for the rest of the afternoon."

He caught the remote Brett threw to him and flicked through the channels until he found a rerun of an old action flick. He rearranged the cushions behind his head and tried not to think of his parents' impending visit.

It's not that they didn't love him, he knew they did in their own way, but he'd never had the hugs and demonstrative affection that he'd witnessed with Brett's family. He'd been shocked the first time he'd gone to Brett's house at aged eleven. Rose and John Parker had welcomed him with open arms and treated him like another son. No, his own parents were caught up in their careers as a university lecturer and lawyer. They'd pushed him to do well at school and had appeared happy when he'd chosen to do his degree in teaching. They'd been disappointed when he said he was going to teach English at secondary school level rather than at a university. Their lack of support had almost made him reconsider, but he didn't want to be compared to his father, who was considered one of the foremost English professors in the country. As hard as the education sector was, Stu got great satisfaction from shaping young teen's minds and preparing them for whatever they wanted to do in the future.

He'd long ago buried the hurt that had plagued him through his teenage years once he'd realised that he was little more than an accessory to their lives. He'd often wondered if they'd only had him because it was the expected norm—get your degree, marry well, have a child. He'd never had the nerve to ask them and didn't really want to know the answer.

Chapter Five

Stu was stretched out on the couch later that week when Brett got home. His new flatmate shuffled past him to the kitchen without acknowledgment to return with a couple of beers, one of which he handed over to Stu.

Sitting up, he took the proffered bottle before settling in the corner of the couch as Brett flopped down tiredly on the other end, resting his head on the back of the seat and closing his eyes. Tension radiated off him.

"Bad day?" Stu asked quietly.

Brett sighed before sitting up and taking a mouthful of beer. "Yeah. Car versus truck in peak hour traffic. Critical injuries and a hell of a mess to clean up."

"You okay?"

"Mmm," Brett hummed. "I will be. I went and did some laps at the pool before coming home. And there'll be a full debrief when I go in tomorrow afternoon." Tiredness and grief darkened Brett's navy-blue eyes. "Y'know, you'd think after doing this job for all of my adult life, I'd be used to things like this now."

"Hey, don't beat yourself up. You do the job because you love it and because you're bloody good at it. Accidents like today get to you because you care. You always have and you always will. The day you don't come home feeling like shit about whatever you've been called out to will be the day to hang up your helmet."

"Yeah, I know," Brett replied before relaxing back into the couch.

"There's some leftover lasagne in the fridge, if you want some for dinner," Stu offered.

A smile spread across Brett's face, even though he didn't open his eyes. "Homemade?"

"Duh. Is that even a question?"

"Well, I know you crusty old cat-men like to buy the readymade frozen meals, y'know, so you don't have to cook for one." Brett sat up fully and grinned.

"I take it back. There's no leftovers whatsoever. Go and cook your own damn dinner." Stu mock huffed, pleased to see his friend relaxing enough to tease.

Brett laughed as he stood and headed into the kitchen. Stu gave a small smile and changed the channel to one of his favourite shows. As expected, he got a groan from Brett when he saw what was on the screen.

"Really? Why do you watch this crap? You know it's nowhere near realistic," he griped as he sat down with his plate of lasagne.

"I know you think it's cheesy, but you know I don't watch it for the story line. I watch it for the hunky firemen with their long hoses," Stu told him with a cheeky wink.

Brett rolled his eyes and started to eat his dinner as they watched the fictional fire crew race off to a burning warehouse.

"Aww, come on. There is no way he'd remove his breathing apparatus in the middle of a burning building. That's just ridiculous," Brett argued, waving his fork at the screen. "The Incident Commander would have my balls if I did something like that."

"Have you never heard of artistic licence? Just suspend your disbelief and eat your dinner."

Brett stayed reasonably quiet for the rest of the show. Stu tried not to laugh every time his friend huffed or tutted at the action on the screen. He gave his own dramatic sigh when the lead actor appeared without his shirt on and burst out laughing when he heard Brett mutter under his breath.

"What was that?" he asked with a grin.

"I said, I've seen better abs in the shower in the morning," Brett replied as he returned his dirty plate to the kitchen.

"That's what I thought you said," Stu called out. He eyed his friend from top to toe when he walked back into the room. "Yeah, you probably could give him a run for his money, but I think his abs are a bit more defined than yours."

Brett looked down at his flat stomach and pulled his t-shirt up, revealing a very nice six pack. "What's wrong with these?" he asked, running his hand across the taut muscles.

Stu found himself tracking the movement, and he couldn't help but acknowledge that his best friend had a great set of abs with a pale blond treasure trail leading down to the waistband of the black sweats he was wearing. His body warmed at the sight, and he shifted position on the couch.

"Hey, my eyes are up here." The sound of Brett's voice pulled him from his staring, and he looked up to find Brett grinning at him. "Like what you see?"

"How could I not," he said airily, trying to cover the fact he'd been affected. "You have a great body. I'd have to be blind not to notice." To his surprise, Brett blushed and quickly dropped his shirt.

"Aww, don't get shy on me now," he teased.

"Shut up and watch your programme," Brett groused back, staring fixedly at the TV.

Stu frowned at his friend. It wasn't like him to act weird at a compliment. Brett was well used to his teasing. He turned his own attention to the screen, putting Brett's weirdness down to him being tired.

*****

Brett sank into the couch and tried to ignore the feeling of awareness that swamped through him at Stu's comment and the way his friend's eyes had lingered on his stomach. He'd almost managed to put out of his mind the events of Saturday night, but Stu's perusal had awakened the memories, and now he was conscious of the other man sitting at the end of the couch.

Stu was wearing a pair of old faded jeans, the denim soft and worn. He had his left leg propped up against the arm of the chair and there was an inch long rip, about a hands-width down the seam from his groin, and Brett had an urge to run his hand up Stuart's thigh and slip a finger into the hole. His fingers gave an involuntary twitch at the thought, and he felt his skin heat again.

He tried to focus on the screen, but the show frustrated him with its lack of realism, and he suppressed a groan when two of the characters started making out in the equipment room. A chuckle from the other end of the couch had him glaring at Stu, who just laughed even louder. With a muttered sigh, Brett stood and headed to the kitchen.

"You want a coffee?" he called out.

"Tea, please."

Brett quickly made the hot drinks and was relieved to see the credits rolling when he returned. After handing Stu his mug, he snatched the remote off the arm of the chair and started flicking through the channels. He settled on a mid-week sports show and it was his turn to chuckle as Stu gave his own groan.

"This is better than that crap you were just watching," he told Stu as highlights from the weekend rugby matches were shown.

"I prefer to be more up close and personal when men are playing with their balls," Stu retorted. The sudden visual of Stu playing with his balls flooding Brett's brain had a prickle of heat run through him and his dick twitching. He shuffled and adjusted the cushion behind him in an attempt to disguise what was happening in his pants. He huffed a laugh and muttered, "I'm sure you do."

From the corner of his eye, he saw Stu give him an odd look.

"You okay over there, B?"

"What? Yeah, sure. Why?" he said, pretending to be absorbed by the discussion on the screen.

"You just seem a bit twitchy, that's all."

"Nah, all good." He nodded to the screen. "So what do you think of these guys' chances this weekend?"

Stu frowned at the subject change before replying. They made small talk about players as Brett tried not to notice every move Stu made. Over the last few days, he'd become more aware of Stu, noticing things he'd never really thought about: how, when engrossed in a book, he unconsciously played with the string on his hoodie, and how he let out a soft gasp when something unexpected happened. More than once he'd noticed how good the other man smelled after a shower.

He was feeling confused and guilty and he didn't know how to deal with it other than to try to will it away. He was sure it was just a phase and this infatuation would soon wear off.

He drained his coffee mug and stood, passing the remote back to Stu as he walked past. Instead of taking the device, Stu's hand closed around Brett's wrist, holding him in place. Brett froze as a tingle ran up his arm.

"Are you sure you're okay?" Stu asked, concerned. "You know you can talk to me anytime, about anything."

Brett nodded. "Yeah, I know. I'm fine, mate. Just need a decent night's sleep."

Stu let go and smiled up at him. "Okay. I suppose I'll see you Friday then. Be safe."

"Always am. You have a good last few days of term and prepare to party on Saturday."

"Looking forward to it already."

"Great. I'll…um…head off to bed then." With a nod, Brett headed for his room, mentally berating himself at his lame behaviour. If he kept this up, Stu would soon figure out something was wrong.

Chapter Six

As Stu let himself into the house, a huge clap of thunder sounded overhead, and a few seconds later a flash of lightning lit up the sky. It looked like it was going to be a miserable night and it matched his mood perfectly.

As expected, lunch with his parents had been hard work. They had asked their usual questions about his career and done little to disguise their disappointment when he told them he was extremely happy where he was and that he had no plans to change schools to a better paying private one or chase the head of department position that had been advertised at another local school.

Walking into the brightly lit kitchen, he stopped short at the sight of the table set with his good china and wine glasses and the smell of his favourite garlic and herb chicken roasting in the oven.

"I thought I heard you come in," Brett said as he appeared behind him. "Sounds like you got home just in time," he added as heavy rain pounded on the roof and the lights flickered as another rumble of thunder rolled through the air.

"It's absolutely miserable out there. This storm gave my parents the perfect excuse to cut lunch short so they could get to the airport in time. They're hoping it doesn't affect their flight as they have a dinner to attend tonight with one of the senior partners from my mother's firm."

"Glad to see where their priorities lie." Brett gave him a sympathetic smile.

Stuart waved away the comment with a shrug. "I'm used to it." He nodded at the table. "So what's all this then?"

To his surprise, a faint blush stained Brett's fair skin.

"I know I said I was going to take you out on the town with the guys, but Jase and Kyle are celebrating their one-year anniversary, Mia is teething so Sarah and Mike are exhausted, and Charlie rang to say that Cooper changed his schedule and his flight should be landing about now, so we aren't seeing him for the next month."

"So, it's just you and me then, for dinner?" he queried.

"Well, we could go out, but this weather is supposed to get worse before it gets better, so I figured I'd cook your favourite meal and we'd have a few drinks and chill out here. The guys and I promise to make it up to you next weekend."

"Actually, this is perfect, B. Thank you." Stu smiled at his best friend. He was quietly relieved that he didn't have to go out again. He was mentally drained after seeing his parents and a quiet night in was just what he needed.

"You're sure? If you want to go out, we can."

"No. This is good. I went out last night with the people from work, so it will be nice to have a quiet one at home."

"Great." Brett beamed at him, and some of the tension from the day eased from Stu's shoulders and he pulled the other man into a quick hug.

"You really are the best friend a guy could have," Stu told him before stepping back and heading to the fridge. "Beer or wine?" he asked. When Brett didn't reply, he glanced over his shoulder to find his friend looking at him oddly. "What?"

"Huh? Oh, nothing. Sorry, beer, thanks. I grabbed a bottle of your favourite wine. It should be chilled enough by now."

Shaking his head at his friend's strange behaviour, he grabbed their drinks from the fridge and opened them.

"Before I forget, happy birthday." Brett shoved an envelope in his hand before taking a drink from his beer.

Stu slipped a finger under the edge of the envelope and removed the card inside. As per tradition, it was rude, and he chuckled at the picture and message about his balls being saggy now he was old. As he opened it, a piece of paper dropped out. He unfolded it and found tickets to the upcoming performance of a Midsummer Night's Dream being put on by the Pop-Up Globe Shakespeare theatre company.

"Wow. How did you manage to get these?" he asked, delighted at the gift.

"Ben at work, his brother is one of the stage crew and he got them for me. It is the one you wanted to see, isn't it?"

"Yes. Any of the plays they're doing this year would be great, but Midsummers is my favourite and I heard they are doing parts of it in Te Reo Maori, which will be a whole new slant on it." Stu grinned at his friend. "Thank you so much. This is the best present ever."

Brett grinned back. "You're welcome. I hope you enjoy it."

Stu carefully tucked the tickets back into the card and laid it on the kitchen bench, before pulling Brett into another hug. "Thanks, mate. You always get me the best gifts."

Brett gave him a pat on the shoulder before drawing away. He seemed embarrassed, which was not like him. Stu frowned as Brett turned away to the oven to check on the chicken. When he turned back, he noticed Brett wouldn't quite meet his eye. Before Stu could say anything though, there was a crack of lightening and the lights flickered before going out.

"Shit," both men said together.

"I'll get the candles," Stu said as he opened the torch app on his phone. Brett did the same and the kitchen lit up enough for them to see what they were doing.

"Maybe we should go out after all."

"No. We'll be fine. I've got some playing cards somewhere; we can amuse ourselves for the evening." Stu began rummaging through one of the kitchen drawers for the candles he kept for such occasions. He looked up at Brett, who was glaring at his phone.

"Come on, mate. It's not the end of the world. There is an emergency kit in the hall cupboard which has the battery lamp in it. Go and grab that and it will save the batteries on our phones."

"I know. I just wanted you to have a great birthday, and first we don't go out because of the weather, and now I can't finish cooking dinner because, you know, no power," Brett said as he pointed at the oven.

"And here I thought you were a practical man, B," Stuart responded with a grin.

Brett frowned at him, not understanding what Stu was getting at.

"We have the barbecue outside on the deck. It's under cover so you won't get wet. All you have to do is stick it on there, close the lid, and let it finish cooking. I doubt it's got long to go, has it?"

A look of relief spread across Brett's features and he nodded in agreement. "I'd forgotten you'd got that outdoor kitchen monstrosity. I'll grab the lamp and get it all fired up."

*****

Candlelight highlighted the slant of Stu's cheekbones and the firm line of his jaw as he looked at the panel of tiles in front of him. Brett gave a mental headshake. He'd thought that not seeing Stu for a few days while at work would have erased the irrational feelings he'd been having. It hadn't though; if anything, it had made things worse. Sure, he'd always acknowledged that Stu was an attractive man, but he'd never wondered what it would be like to run his fingers along the stubble-roughened skin. Never wondered if he tasted as good as he smelt.

Stu looked up and caught him staring. He raised an eyebrow. "What's that look for?"

"Just wondering what word you're about to play. No doubt it will be something obscure and you'll manage to land it on the triple-word score as well," Brett said wryly. They'd pulled out the battered Scrabble board and so far, Brett had lost two games and had only just broken over one hundred both times. He wasn't faring much better this game either.

"I could say I'm sorry, but I'm not. Besides, it's my birthday, so you have to let me win," Stu told him as he carefully laid his tiles onto the board. "I think you'll find that gives me a total of thirty-six and that means I'm now on one hundred and eighty-four."

"Frottage? That's not a legal word," Brett protested. Picking up his beer, he drained the remainder and pushed out of his chair.

"It is a legal word. It means…"

"I know what it means. I just don't think it's legal. I thought it was slang." He pulled the fridge door open. "Want a top up?" he asked, waving the almost empty wine bottle at Stu.

"Yeah, may as well finish it."

Brett returned to the table and poured the remainder of the wine into Stu's glass before sitting down and twisting the cap of his beer.

"Thanks. No, frottage is okay, but the word frotting isn't allowed," Stu informed him with a grin.

"Whatever. Of course you'd know that. You're beating the pants off me. I don't know why I bother," Brett grumbled good naturedly.

"Oooh. There's an idea." Mischief lit Stu's eyes, making them dance as he looked over the rim of his glass.

"Oh, fuck. Now what have you thought of?"

"Strip Scrabble." Stu leaned back in his chair, his eyes widening as the idea grew in his mind. "Why have I never thought of that before?"

Brett groaned. "We are *not* playing strip Scrabble. In twenty years of knowing you, I've only ever beaten you twice, and I'm sure you let me win both times."

"Maybe." Stu shrugged distractedly as his eyes lit up again. "One of the rules could be if the word played lands on a double or triple word score, the loser has to take off two or three items of clothing."

"It would be easier for me just to play naked then. You'd have me stripped in ten minutes. Where would the fun be in that?"

Stu gave him a lazy look, his gaze travelling up and down Brett's body, and his blue eyes darkened. The air between them thickened as Brett's skin prickled at the way Stu was looking at him. Stu's tongue flicked out and swiped along his bottom lip, making it glisten in the candlelight, and Brett had a sudden urge to taste those full lips.

Stu put his wine glass down and leaned across the table, his eyes never leaving Brett's. "Don't you know that the tease and anticipation is half the fun?" he asked huskily.

"What?" Brett had lost track of what they were talking about.

"It would be no fun playing naked. The tease and anticipation of someone stripping is what makes it so much more enjoyable."

"Ah…um…yeah. I s'pose it is," Brett stammered as his mind filled with images of Stu stripping for him and then the familiar feeling of guilt for even picturing his best friend like that.

Stu was watching him, an unreadable look on his face. He opened his mouth to say something when a click and whir sounded, and the room was suddenly filled with bright light as the power came back on.

Both men gave a start as the moment was shattered. They looked at each other briefly before Brett stood, blowing out the candles.

"I think I'm...um…going to call it a night," he told Stu as he ran a shaking hand through his hair.

"Hang on a sec, B." Stu got up from the table and stood in front of him. "Thanks for tonight. It's one of the nicest birthdays I've had."

"It's the least I could do. You're my best mate. I'm just sorry it didn't go as we'd planned."

"No, I mean it." Stuart placed a palm on Brett's bicep and leaned forward. Brett froze, not daring to move. A warm kiss pressed against his cheek. As Stu stepped back, Brett let out the breath he'd been holding.

"What's wrong?" Stu asked with a tilt of his head, eyes searching Brett's face.

"Noth-nothing. You took me by surprise that's all," Brett told him, forcing out a chuckle.

"B, I've kissed you on the cheek before. You've been weird all week. What's going on?"

"No I haven't, and nothing's going on."

"Er, yes, you have. Have I made you uncomfortable somehow? You've never minded me hugging you before."

"Now you're being weird." Brett rolled his eyes. "Come here." He tugged Stu into a warm hug, trying to keep his body relaxed. Stu's scent wrapped around him, and he took in a deep breath of lime and peppermint. As they pulled apart, the rasp of stubble scraping along his own sent tingles down his spine.

"Thanks again. I'll put the dishwasher on. I'll see you in the morning." Stu gave him a faint smile and moved towards the kitchen.

"Yeah. Night, Stu. See you in the morning."

Brett escaped to his room and leaned against the door, letting out a long sigh. *Fuck.* This infatuation was going to have to stop. He'd struggled to not pull Stu in for a tighter hug just then. He'd wanted to turn his head and capture Stu's mouth and see if it was as soft as it looked. The thought of making out had his body warming, and he pressed a hand against his thickening cock. *No, he was NOT going to jack off to thoughts of his best mate—again.*

Pushing away from the door, he stripped off and climbed into bed. He put his earbuds in and tapped into a playlist, hoping the music would lull him to sleep.

Chapter Seven

As Brett passed Charlie a mug of coffee, he heard the familiar clatter of keys in the front door. Brett sat down at the dining table and grinned as Stu's footsteps faltered as he entered the living room. Stu looked at his couch and then up at a grinning Brett and Charlie.

"Oh, Charlie, you shouldn't have," Stuart quipped as he leaned on the sofa back, taking his fill of the stretched-out form sprawled across the cushions. "I know you love me, but giving me your worn out boyfriend for my birthday is really just too much."

"He's in perfect working order, just a little …" Charlie paused, his face scrunching as he pretended to think of the right word.

"Shagged out?" offered Brett.

"Broken?" suggested Stu.

The three men laughed as a growl sounded from the couch. "I'm fuckin' jet-lagged, you arse-holes."

"So, you *are* giving him to me for my birthday?" Stu teased as he made his way over to the table.

"Stu, mate. As much as I do love you, no. Never. Not in this lifetime. Nada." Charlie looked fondly at Cooper, who was now sitting up and pushing his long hair out of his face.

Cooper returned the look, and Brett felt a twinge of envy that they could be so open with each other.

"Not that I'm not pleased to see you both, but why are you here? I didn't expect to see you guys for at least a month as you reacquainted yourselves," Stu commented.

"That was my plan," Cooper replied as he joined them at the table. He gave Stu a hug before continuing. "But the bossy builder over there said we had to come and choose tiles today. Tiles! Haven't seen him for over two months and all he wants to do is go fuckin' shopping."

"If the picky rock star owner of the house I'm *trying* to renovate had decided on said tiles a month ago when he was asked, we would be at home in bed right now, *not* rushing around town making last minute orders so they are here before Christmas," Charlie shot back with a mock-glare.

"Well, excuse me! I've only been a little bit busy putting together the best album of my life and promoting the hell out of it so I can pay for the renovations. I told you to pick what you liked as you'll be living there too."

Charlie glowered at Cooper before his mouth twitched. He let out a huff, trying to maintain a serious façade.

Brett snorted and glanced at Stu, who was doing his best to hold his laugh in as well. Catching each other's eye, they burst into peals of laughter, which Charlie and Cooper joined in.

"You pair are like an old married couple already," Stu wheezed between laughs.

"Anyway, tile shopping wasn't the only reason we're here. We stopped in to wish you a happy birthday—albeit a belated one—and also for Coop to catch up with you guys."

"Yeah, did you have a good birthday?" Cooper asked.

Stu nodded as he filled them in on their evening. "I came up with a great new game idea too," he declared with a grin.

"No. You didn't. It was a crap idea." Brett groaned.

"You're just a prude. It is *so* such a good game idea."

"Am not a prude. I just don't think Strip Scrabble would catch on."

"You two sound like you're the old married couple," Charlie muttered before he took a sip from his coffee.

Cooper grinned in agreement, and Brett rolled his eyes and pushed away from the table.

"Coop, you want that cup of tea now you're awake?"

"Yes please." Cooper turned to Stu. "So, tell me more about this game."

Brett flicked the kettle on and began preparing tea for Cooper. He dropped a coffee pod into the machine and made Stu one while he was waiting.

"Any luck with finding a new place to live, Brett?" Charlie asked him as he returned to the table with the mugs.

"Not really," Brett told him. "To be honest, I haven't looked that much. I've more or less decided I want a studio flat. I'm over living with flatmates. It's hard to find ones that get the whole shift work thing."

"You know you are more than welcome to use either Lizzie's or Carl's places," Charlie offered. "Both are busy in England and their cottages are just sitting there looking pretty. They'd only charge a nominal rent."

"Thanks, mate. I'd love to, but the forty-minute drive each way is a bit of a deal breaker."

"Fair enough, but the offer is there for when Stu gets sick of you and you have nowhere else."

Brett nodded his thanks. He really had to start looking for a place of his own. He knew Stu would never kick him out, but he didn't want to overstay his welcome. Part of his problem was that he was too comfortable. It felt more like home than any other place he'd stayed, including when he'd lived with Louise. He'd always felt that it was her place, not theirs. He'd not felt that with Stu. They'd slipped into an easy routine that was grounded in a long familiarity with each other. They worked well together, and the more Brett thought about moving out, the less he wanted to.

"Apart from the…um…picky owner"—Brett winked at Cooper—"how are the renos coming along?"

"Not too bad, but if you're free on your next days off, I'd love the help," Charlie said.

"I'm helping," Cooper protested. "Or, at least, I will be when you let me out of your bed."

"Really? That's the excuse you're going with?" Charlie said with an eye roll. Cooper bat his eyes at Charlie, who shook his head at his boyfriend's antics. "Come on then. Let's go home so we can get back to work."

"Something will get nailed," Stuart said dryly. "And I'm sure wood will be involved too."

Cooper laughed and pulled Stu into another hug. "Oh, I have missed you. You guys must come out for dinner one night, and we can have a few beers and maybe a round or two of strip Scrabble."

"We'd love to." Stuart returned the embrace.

Brett felt that twinge of envy again as Charlie grabbed Cooper's hand and twined their fingers together. He'd never had that: the easy touch and soft glances. Even with Louise. She'd held his hand or would slip an arm around his waist, but they'd never been as in-sync as Cooper and Charlie were, or even Jase and Kyle, when he thought about it.

"I'll call you next week, Brett. Let me know what days you have off and are available. If you know any guys that might want a bit of extra cash and recognise one end of a hammer from the other, then give them my number."

"Thanks, Charlie. I'll mention it at the station tomorrow."

They said their goodbyes, and Brett began tidying up the used coffee mugs.

"I don't think I've ever seen Charlie so happy," Stu commented as he came back into the room.

"Yeah. It's good to see." Brett closed the dishwasher before looking at Stu. "Do you think you'll ever find someone? Y'know, like Charlie and Jase have?"

"Nah. Like I said the other week, I'm happy being single. If I get an itch, I can get someone to scratch it. I'll leave the whole love and forever thing to you guys." Stu gave him a quizzical stare. "What about you? Are you ready to get back in the dating game?"

"Maybe? When I see how easy Charlie and Cooper make it look, then yeah, I want that. I want someone who knows me inside out."

"They haven't had it easy though, B. You know that. Remember how miserable Charlie was when Coop was in England? And that was even knowing it was only for a few months. They've had to work hard to get where they are and make some big compromises along the way. They deserve what they've got because they worked so hard for it."

Brett raked a hand through his hair. "What I mean is that I want to find that one person who makes all that effort worth it."

"Well, to do that, you need to actually go out and meet someone. Get back on the horse."

"I know, but…"

"There is no but. You either put the work in to find someone, or you join me in happy bachelorhood. We need to go out on the town and find you someone. Or you could use a dating app." Stu paused as he thought and then snapped his fingers. "I've got it. You could apply to that reality show. You know, the one where you meet your bride at the altar."

"What? No way in fucking hell. Have you seen the train wrecks they try to pass off as relationships?"

"Not all of them are. Those guys that got fake married on Valentine's Day? They stayed together, and I read in the paper that they've just become engaged for real. So sometimes it does work out."

"Nope. I'd rather play strip Scrabble with a bunch of naked guys than sign up to any reality TV show."

"Well, that can easily be arranged."

"Fuck off, Stu."

"Love you too, B."

Chapter Eight

A light rain spattered on their shoulders as Brett and Stu dashed from the taxi to the entrance of The Smoking Keg. The city bar was packed, and they could hear a loud bass pumping from the street. There was a sizeable crowd inside, and the mass of bodies gave off a welcome warmth after the chill of the outside air.

"Didn't expect it to be this busy," Brett shouted in Stu's ear as he shook the dampness from his hair.

"It's good. Means there's more bodies to choose from." Stu gave him a filthy grin and winked.

"Just remember to text me before you bugger off with someone, okay?" Brett pleaded. He was regretting this idea of bringing Stu out on the town. He wasn't sure he wanted to have Stu hook up with someone and then bring them home. He couldn't face a repeat of a few weeks ago.

Stu nodded before heading to the bar and squeezing between two guys waiting to be served. They both looked at him and threw him flirty grins. Brett watched as his friend gave them both a quick once over, grinning back before catching the attention of the bartender. One of the guys leaned over and said something that caused Stuart to laugh and shake his head. He replied to the guy before paying for their drinks and returning to Brett.

"Thanks." Brett took the proffered beer and swallowed a mouthful. "That must be a record for you," he commented.

"What must be?

"The guy at the bar. I saw how he looked at you. Did he ask for your number?" Brett replied with a grin and a quirk of his eyebrow.

Stu's face lit up as he laughed. "Nah, mate. He was asking if you were with me."

Brett frowned, causing Stu to laugh harder. He glanced over his shoulder and jolted as the guy in question raised his bottle in salute and gave Brett a wink. "Wait, you mean, with you as in *with* you?"

"Yes. Don't look so worried. I set him straight, so to speak. It's not like it's the first time people have thought we're a couple." Stuart patted him on the shoulder. "Come on, let's see if we can find you someone more suited to your tastes."

The Smoking Keg was one of the largest bars on the Viaduct Harbour with bifold doors that opened out to a view of the moored superyachts taking up almost one side. The serving area ran the length of the back wall and there was a good-sized dance floor to the right, with the DJ booth on a slightly raised platform overlooking the area. Dotted around were leaner tables and two small private booths tucked in the back corner. It was very LGBTQ friendly and there were people of all orientations and genders dancing and partying. It was a favourite hangout for them and their friends as it was safe and comfortable for all. Stu had invited the rest of the gang to come out, but they had all had other things planned, so it was just the two of them tonight.

It didn't take long for Stu to disappear onto the dance floor and he was soon grinding between two other guys, their bodies moving perfectly to the pounding beat. Feeling slightly abandoned, Brett dragged his gaze away and looked around the crowd. He spotted a pretty brunette who smiled at him shyly when he caught her eye. He smiled back at her and nodded towards the dancers. She blushed, and her friend gave her a slight nudge before she nodded. Brett left his empty beer bottle on the tall table he had been leaning against and headed over to her.

"Hi," he said as he got close enough to be heard. "Want to dance?"

"Yeah, sure."

They squeezed onto the crowded floor and were soon moving in time to the beat. She was a good dancer, and as she relaxed, her smile got a little brighter.

Brett introduced himself, shouting over the music to be heard.

"Lucy," she replied with a smile. Brett reached out and took her hand in his, pulling her closer, before dropping the other to her hip. She peered up at him through her lashes and laid her palm on his chest. She wasn't tall, her head coming to just past Brett's chin, and he could smell her light perfume. Flawless makeup highlighted smooth skin and her lips were a deep red.

Brett glanced up and spotted Stu, who was now wrapped around a tall, dark-haired guy. He tried not to stare, pushing away the twinge of jealousy that hit him. A tug on his hand had his attention returning to Lucy, and he gave her what he hoped was a convincing smile.

Brett danced with Lucy for a while longer before asking if she wanted a drink. She nodded and, slipping his palm into hers, he led her off the dance floor towards the bar.

She pointed to her friends, and he nodded, letting go of her. "I'm just going to the bathroom and then I'll meet you back here," he told her.

"Okay, thanks."

A few minutes later Brett was back trying to spot Lucy and her companions. As he scanned the crowd, he saw a familiar blond head and recognised Stu disappearing into a darkened corner with the guy he'd been dancing with. He quickly dismissed a feeling of dejection as a tap on his shoulder had him turning to find Lucy smiling at him shyly. Next to her was her friend, who was looking a little glassy eyed and weaving slightly in the three-inch stilettos she was wearing.

"I'm really sorry, Brett, but I need to leave and get Candice home. She's had a bit too much to drink, and I don't want her to try to make her way on her own."

"Heee's pretty," Candice slurred as she ran a hand down Brett's arm. "Why're you sooo pretty?"

Brett chuckled as Lucy rolled her eyes. "Now you know why I need to take her home."

"No worries. It was nice meeting you. Are you okay to find a ride?"

"Yes. I've already called an Uber, so we should head out." She gave him a sweet smile. "Thanks for the dance. Enjoy the rest of your night." With a small wave, she took her friend by the elbow and began steering her towards the door.

Disappointed, Brett headed to the bar and ordered another beer. His enthusiasm for the night had left him and although he knew he could find someone else to dance with, he just wanted to go home. He tried to catch the eye of one of the bartenders and jumped when a firm hand landed on his shoulder. "Hey, sexy, come here often?" a deep voice spoke in his ear, and he turned to find the grinning faces of Jase and Kyle.

"If that's the line you used to pick up Kyle, he must have been drunker than I thought," Brett said with a laugh as he was pulled into a hug, first by Jase and then by Kyle.

"He didn't need a line. His ass did all the talking for him." Kyle winked as he ran an appreciative hand over Jase's jeans-clad backside.

Brett peered over Jase's shoulder. "Yeah. I can understand that."

"Brett Parker! Since when have you been an admirer of men's arses?" Jase asked as he leaned into Kyle's embrace.

"Just because I don't partake, doesn't mean I can't appreciate fineness when I see it," Brett retorted. "Anyway, what are you two doing here? I thought you had plans?"

"We were going to have dinner with my sister and her new boyfriend, but he got free tickets to some concert that's on, and they cancelled on us, so we decided to come and see if we could find you." Jase scanned the crowd. "Where's Stu?"

"Last seen heading into the far corner attached to a bloke." Brett indicated with his bottle the vague direction he'd seen Stu disappearing to.

"And you've not found anyone?" Kyle asked as he passed Jase a beer.

"Yeah, I was dancing with a girl, but she had to take her friend home who was a little tipsy."

"Plenty more fish in the sea," Jase told him as he clinked his bottle against Brett's in a mock toast.

Brett nodded his agreement but as the night wore on, he noticed that although there were lots of beautiful women there, many who expressed their interest, Brett found himself constantly searching for a certain blond.

*****

Pushing his way through the crowd, Stu kept an eye out for Brett and the guys. He'd picked up a text from Brett earlier that Jase and Kyle had joined them. He quickly scanned the area around the bar as he drank down half a bottle of water. Dancing had been fun but hot. He needed a few minutes to cool down. From the corner of his eye, he caught sight of the trio leaning against a tall table, and he made his way over to them.

Brett was against the wall, one hand clutching a beer, the other tucked into the pocket of his jeans. A lazy smile spread across his features as he spotted Stu, and

Stu recognised the signs of a comfortable buzz. Squeezing between the table and the wall, Stu gave Brett a friendly shoulder nudge before greeting Jase and Kyle.

"Thought you'd be off for the night," Jase said.

"I thought so too, but his recent ex turned up and it started getting a bit too messy for me, so I bailed." Stu took a deep drink from the chilled water.

"We're about to head off, but we didn't want to leave Brett on his own. He's had a few tonight," Kyle said as he slipped an arm around Jase, pulling him tight into his body.

"You guys go. I'll take him home. I'm surprised he's drunk though. He's usually the responsible one when we go out."

"He struck out with some girl earlier, so I think he's drowning his sorrows."

Stu glanced at his friend and noticed Brett watching him as though he was trying to figure something out.

"Come on, B. Let's get you home." Stu slipped an arm around Brett's shoulders and tugged him upright.

"S'okay. I'm fine. I can walk," Brett grumbled and promptly stumbled as he got clear of the table.

His companions laughed as Stu gently guided them towards the door. Once outside in the cool fresh air, Brett swayed alarmingly, and Stu quickly grasped him around the waist. Brett leaned heavily into him as he slung an arm around Stu's neck.

"Sure you're okay to get him home?" Jase asked with concern.

"Yeah." Stu sighed. "We've done this dance before. I've got him. You guys go, and we'll see you tomorrow for brunch."

Jase and Kyle left with a wave, and Stu dragged Brett towards a waiting taxi. With a bit of manoeuvring, he wrangled his friend into the car before slipping in next to him. He gave the driver his address and rested back on the seat. Brett gave a deep sigh and his head fell onto Stu's shoulder.

"You okay, mate?" Stu asked him with a quiet chuckle.

Brett's hand landed on his thigh and began to rub up and down the denim. "You look good in these jeans, but I prefer the ones with the hole in them."

"What jeans with the hole in them?"

"Y'know. The sexy ones. They've got a hole…right…there." As Brett said the last word, he stabbed a finger on Stu's left inseam.

Stu froze as Brett scratched at his leg, mid-thigh. Sensation shot through him and he willed himself not to react. He gently took the wandering hand and placed it back in its owner's lap. "How much have you had to drink tonight, B?"

"A few. I'm not pissed. I'm just not really s…s…sober," Brett slurred, and his hand returned to Stu's leg and began rubbing again. "It's a lot harder, y'know. But then I s'pose it's gonna be, isn't it?"

"What are you talking about, B? What's a lot harder?" Stu took a calming breath, trying to ignore the sensations that were making certain parts of him hard.

"A guy's leg. I mean, y'know, a girl's thigh is soft, but yours is hard. And firm." Brett gave him a squeeze just above his knee, and Stu jerked as pain radiated sharply through his leg.

"Don't fucking do that," he growled out, grabbing Brett's hand and pushing it away, the pressure aggravating an old soccer injury. Massaging his thigh to disperse the pain that had quickly deflated his semi. Which was an upside, but on the downside, there was a chance he'd be limping when he got out of the car.

"Oh, shit. Sorry, mate. Forgot that was your bad knee. Wan' me to kiss it better?" Brett lurched forward, his face heading towards Stu's lap. Stuart grabbed him by the shoulders and pushed him back to the other side of the cab.

"What the *fuck* has got into you tonight?"

Navy blue eyes stared back at him, wide and confused. "Sor…sorry." Brett's head slumped against the window and he closed his eyes as though hiding from Stu's gaze.

Stu softened his tone, feeling bad for his friend. "It's okay, mate. You took me by surprise. Come on, we're home. Let's get you inside and into bed."

Stu thanked the driver and hauled Brett from the cab. He kept one hand on the other man's shoulder to keep him steady, but Brett shrugged it off and navigated the short path to the front door on his own.

After letting them in, he dropped his keys onto the small hall table. Brett still wasn't looking at him and began shuffling down the hallway, tension riding his shoulders. Now that the shock had worn off, Stu chuckled to himself. Brett would *hate* himself in the morning for giving Stu so much teasing fodder for months, if not years, to come. Taking pity on his friend, he called out, "Hey, B, go to bed. I'll bring you some water."

Grabbing two bottles of water from the fridge, he was still smiling to himself when he turned to find Brett standing a few feet away from him. "I told you I'd bring it to you," he said as he handed the bottle over.

Brett took it but didn't open it, instead placing it on the kitchen counter, not breaking eye contact.

"What's up, B? Are you feeling okay?" Stu was unsure of Brett's mood. His best friend was usually a happy drunk, but tonight he was acting strangely.

"Why didn't you go home with the guy you were with?" Brett asked, crossing his arms over his chest.

"Um…I told you. His ex turned up, and I didn't want to be part of any lover's spat. Why?" Stu wondered where his friend was heading.

"Was he a good kisser?"

Stu blinked, not sure if he'd heard right. "What?"

"Was he a good kisser?" Brett asked as though the fate of the world rested on his answer.

"He was okay," Stu replied with a shrug. The two kisses he'd managed before the other guy's ex had shown up hadn't been bad. He'd certainly had worse.

"I know you'd be a great kisser," Brett said knowingly with a firm nod.

"You do? How do you know that?" Amused by the turn in conversation, Stu relaxed back against the fridge. Oh dear, Brett was *really* going to hate himself in the morning.

"You've got a great looking mouth. Your bottom lip especially. It looks perfect for nibbling on." Brett's gaze dropped to Stu's mouth and he licked his own lips before meeting Stu's eyes again, as if daring him to disagree.

Stu froze as Brett moved a step closer, reaching out a tentative hand before dropping it back to his side. Stu straightened from his slouch so they were almost eye to eye. Brett's extra two inches in height meant Stu had to lift his chin slightly.

He searched Brett's face for a clue as to what he might be thinking. His own mind was racing. Where had this all come from? In all the years they had been friends, Brett had never once expressed an interest in him, or even men in general.

"Do you want to kiss me, B?" he asked quietly, watching carefully for a reaction.

"Yes. No. I don't know," Brett said, confusion clearly written on his face. He shoved his hands into his jean pockets, took them out again, crossed his arms.

"Talk to me, Brett. What's going through your head right now?" Stu laid a reassuring hand on Brett's shoulder, which twitched under his touch.

"I don't know, Stu. I've been noticing things and I don't understand what it all means." Pleading eyes met Stu's.

"What have you been noticing?"

Brett waved a hand up and down, gesturing towards Stuart.

"You've been noticing things about…me?"

Brett didn't look at him, just gave a small nod before hunching in on himself, trying to hide from Stu's scrutiny. Stu had never seen him like this before.

"What…what kind of things have you been noticing?" Stu stumbled over the words, curiosity scrambling his brain as it flitted from one scenario to another. Did Brett mean what he thought he meant?

"Likehowsexyyourjeansare" Brett rushed out in one big breath, still not looking up. A blush flooded his face and he jammed his hands into the back pockets of his jeans.

"You think my jeans are sexy?" Stu asked, looking down at the dark denim he was wearing.

"Not those, the other ones, the ones with the holes." Brett's voice was barely above a whisper now, and Stu had to lean forward to hear him.

"The ones with the holes?" Stu racked his brain. Brett had mentioned something about a hole in his jeans when they were in the taxi. Understanding dawned when he remembered his oldest pair of jeans. He'd had them for years. The denim was faded and soft, and they moulded to his body like a second skin and were his favourite for relaxing in. And yes, they did have a few holes in them.

"Oh, I know which ones you mean," he said with a chuckle. Brett didn't reply.

"Do I make you uncomfortable when I wear them? he probed.

Brett did a half shrug, shake of his head combo that left Stu none the wiser.

"B, talk to me. I'm trying to understand what's going through your head, but I need more information."

Brett glanced at him briefly from beneath his lashes and a soft gasp caught in Stu's chest at the combined look of vulnerable adorability and downright sexiness. Awareness skittered warmly down his spine.

"I...I...Seeing you in those jeans makes me want to...want to..." Brett's voice tailed off.

"Okaaayy." Stu stretched the word out as he marshalled his thoughts. "I know you've had a few drinks, but I don't think you're completely unaware. You've had just enough to give you the courage to voice your thoughts, haven't you?"

There was no reply. Stu bit back his frustration. They'd never had any problems talking, and Brett was clamming up tighter than a virgin on a first date. Stu was obviously going to have to take the lead here as Brett certainly wasn't going to offer any insights voluntarily.

"You're really not helping me here, B, but I'm not going to force you answer any questions or tell me anything you don't want to. I don't want to embarrass you or make you feel uncomfortable. We can forget this conversation ever happened."

Brett ran an agitated hand through his hair. He looked like he was arguing with himself internally. He huffed a sigh, took a step back, took another breath, and exhaled loudly.

"For the last few weeks I've been wondering what it would be like to be with a guy. I've been having dreams and then the other night when you were in those fucking jeans, all I wanted to do was poke a finger in the fucking hole and see how far I could reach up your thigh."

"Gah…" Words failed Stu. In his wildest dreams he'd never expected Brett to say that. Brett was looking at him nervously, but Stu couldn't find the right words to say. "I…ah…um…wasn't…"

"Yeah. Sorry. Didn't mean to embarrass you. I'll go to bed," Brett broke across his stammering. "Just forget it, mate."

"No, wait, B," Stu said, grabbing his arm before he could turn away. "You didn't embarrass me, just surprised me, that's all. Just give me a sec to process this."

Brett gave a quick nod and grabbed his bottle of water, opening it quickly and downing a mouthful. Stu's eyes were drawn to the bob of his Adam's apple and, again, awareness ran through him. He wondered what Brett's skin would taste like, then he shook the thought away. *No, he wasn't going there.* But why not? Brett was obviously curious, and Stu had to admit he was too. Twenty years ago, he'd have given anything to have the opportunity to kiss him. Did he take the opportunity now to find out if it would be as good as he'd always imagined?

"You didn't embarrass me. I'm flattered." He winked to lighten the mood, which elicited an eye roll in return. "If you're curious about kissing and maybe touching, I'm happy to be your guinea pig," he offered rashly, his mouth operating independently to his brain which was swirling with a maelstrom of emotion.

Brett's eyes widened in surprise and a tide of colour flushed his face. His tongue flicked out and swiped along his bottom lip. Stu had a sudden urge to chase that tongue with his own.

"I…um…I…" It was Brett's turn to stammer as he put down the bottle of water. He ran his hand through his hair, making it stand on end.

Stu chuckled. "You look a little stunned, B. It's okay if you don't want to. I won't be offended."

"No, I think I want to."

"Maybe that's your problem." At Brett's raised eyebrow, Stu continued. "Too much thinking. Either you want to know what it's like to kiss a guy or you don't. If you do, you have a perfectly willing subject here, but be quick, it's a limited time offer."

"I do," Brett confirmed. "Are you sure, though?"

"Mate. If this is how you are with a woman before you kiss her, it's no wonder you're single," Stu told him with a roll of his eyes. "Stop overthinking it. If you want to know what it's like to kiss me, then for fuck's sake, just ki—"

Stu was cut off by warm lips pressing against his own and a firm hand at his neck. He held himself still as he waited to see what Brett would do next. This was his experiment, and Stu would follow Brett's lead.

"Damn. If I'd known the best way to shut you up was to kiss you, I would have done it years ago," Brett murmured against his mouth.

Before Stu could offer a smart remark in response, Brett cupped his jaw and looked into his eyes, uncertainty warring with the unspoken question in them. With a small nod, he gave Brett permission to carry on.

This time, Brett's tongue traced along Stuart's bottom lip, teasing it before fitting his mouth against Stu's. There was a brief pause before Brett pulled away slightly and angled his head, pressing back in again. Another swipe of his tongue had Stu parting his lips, and Brett increased the pressure as he began to explore Stu's mouth. It was tentative at first, and Stu responded in kind, gently coaxing Brett to relax.

He flicked his own tongue gently against the one stroking against his lip and a whimper came from Brett as he deepened the kiss. He could taste the beer that Brett had drunk along with a spiciness that seemed to be all his own. A hand traced his ribs before settling at the small of his back, thumb stroking along the edge of his waistband.

Stu unconsciously pulled Brett's hips towards his own before sliding a hand up Brett's arm, feeling the corded muscles flex and tense as his fingers moved from the coarse hairs at the wrist to the smooth cotton of shirt sleeve. Stu silently cursed the material as he wanted to feel the skin that he knew would smooth out farther up Brett's arm.

Brett's hand slipped around Stu's neck and he was tugged closer as Brett's tongue thrust deeper. Heat coursed through Stu's veins as he met Brett kiss for kiss. He loved kissing, always had. He loved soft gentle kisses to strong demanding ones and everything in between. He knew he had to slow this down, though, before he started rubbing against Brett's thigh.

He didn't think Brett was ready for that.

Stu reluctantly eased away from the hot mouth devouring his, pressing kisses along the roughly stubbled jaw and down Brett's throat, giving in to temptation to swipe a lick over his Adam's apple. The tang of light sweat and musk raised goosebumps down his spine. Brett shivered and tucked his face into Stu's shoulder. Their chests heaving slowly against each other as they caught their breaths, Stu slid his fingers into Brett's hair, gently pulling him up from his shoulder. He searched the dazed face of his oldest friend for a reaction before giving one last soft kiss.

"You okay?" he whispered, feeling a little dazed himself. Brett may not have kissed a man before, but he certainly wasn't lacking in skill.

"Yeah. Wow. Um…I feel like I should say thanks, but I know that's not the right thing to say now."

Stu chuckled and pushed Brett back so they had breathing space. "You're welcome. Not that any thanks are required. That was one hot kiss there, Mr Parker." He laughed as Brett blushed. "Surely you've been told you're a great kisser before, B?"

"You're not so bad yourself," Brett retorted, and Stu felt an unfamiliar glow of pleasure.

"So you liked it then? Enough to do it again?"

"It was…different, but at the same time, not."

"So, now you've kissed a guy, has it answered any questions?"

"Maybe? I…I don't know," Brett admitted, his relaxed stance disappearing.

"B. You don't have to work it all out right now. Go to bed, sleep on it, and see how you feel in the morning," Stu said to him warmly.

Brett half nodded in agreement. As Stu left the kitchen, he couldn't help but add, "If you need a refresher, let me know." He laughed as Brett's eyes widened in surprise. "Night, B. Sweet dreams!"

Stu didn't hear the grumbled reply as he closed his bedroom door. Quickly stripping out of his clothes, he collapsed into his bed. The night had definitely not turned out how he'd imagined. He'd thought he'd go out, pick a guy up, and have some fun. Instead, he'd had a few dances and kisses with a stranger, and then come home to an unexpected conversation and a hotter than hell kiss with his best friend. His straight best friend, who now may not be as straight as he thought he was.

Thumping his pillow into shape, he tried to settle into sleep, but the kiss kept replaying through his mind like a video stuck on a continuous loop. His cock lay heavy against his thigh, more than half hard at the memory. He rolled onto his side and shoved his hands under the pillow to stop himself from reaching between his legs. It would be so easy to get off to thoughts of the kiss, but guilt stopped him.

Shit! He'd kissed his best friend, or rather, he'd encouraged his best friend to kiss him. The long-buried memory of his teenage crush flooded back. As much as he'd fancied his best friend in their teen years, he'd also learned to hide it and eventually tuck it to the back of his mind. First rule of gay club: don't fall for your straight best friend.

He was older and wiser now, though. It was just a one-off thing. B would wake up feeling embarrassed for the way he'd behaved, and they'd laugh and then never talk about it again. As sleep crept over him, he didn't examine too closely why that thought made him sad.

Chapter Nine

The weight of Stu's gaze rested on Brett as they ate dinner. Rather than meet his friends eye, he focussed on his plate. He'd managed to avoid Stu for four days by disappearing early on Sunday to Charlie's and then coming home late last night before starting his shift rotation that day. Arriving home from work, he had found dinner cooked and the table set for two. He knew he couldn't escape anymore and decided to eat before facing the inevitable conversation.

He managed to force down the delicate fettucine dish, even as his stomach churned with nerves. Taking the last mouthful, he looked up and caught Stu staring at him.

"Have I got something on my face?" Brett asked, rubbing a hand across his chin as he reached for his beer with the other.

"No."

"So what's the look for, then?" he asked, leaning back in his chair, determined not to be the one who started this conversation.

"Didn't realise I was giving you a look. I was just…looking." Stu took another sip of wine. "How are things with you? Work okay today?"

Brett nodded. "Yeah. Couple of call outs. Lots of paperwork. The usual."

Stu nodded back, trying to appear nonchalant, but his shoulders were tense and his face a bland mask, no twinkle of mischief in the usually expressive blue eyes.

"Thanks for cooking dinner," Brett offered and stood to clear the table.

"No problem," Stu replied as he followed Brett into the kitchen. After rinsing his plate, Stu put it into the dishwasher before refilling his glass of wine and picking up his Kindle off the counter, heading towards the lounge.

Brett took a deep breath. Time to face the music. "Um, Stu."

Stu paused in the doorway and glanced to where Brett was leaning against the kitchen bench.

"What's up?" he asked.

"Can we talk, y'know, about the other night?" Brett ran a nervous hand around the back of his neck as he looked at his friend and gave a tentative smile.

"Sure. Of course." Stu shrugged. Brett could see he was trying to act casual as he led the way into the lounge and sat in his usual spot at the far side of the couch. Brett took the other end and faced him, hands twisting in his lap. Before Brett could start, Stu spoke.

"Mate, stop stressing. It was a simple kiss, and although I was surprised, I'm not upset or anything."

Brett could see that Stu was trying to put him at ease even though tension showed in the lines in his face. Brett nodded in acknowledgement.

"I didn't think you were, but I still need to apologise to you."

"Apologise? What for?" Stuart's brow wrinkled in confusion.

"My behaviour in the taxi, kissing you, and then for avoiding you for the last three days."

"As I said, I was surprised, but you don't need to apologise for that. Ghosting me since then? Well, yes, you do need to say sorry for that." Of course Stu wasn't going to let him off the hook that easily.

"Yeah. I know. I panicked and didn't know how to react. I'm sorry, mate."

"B, we've been friends for too long for something like this affect us. Running off to work for Charlie all week won't save you. You know you can talk to me about anything. Like I said on Saturday night, I was happy for you to experiment on me. You're not the first curious guy I've helped."

"I'm not?"

Stu shook his head. "You'd be surprised how many guys out there wonder what it would be like to be with another man. Even more so now with society being more accepting of sexuality and gender identification."

Brett wasn't sure what to do with that information. He felt a little relief he wasn't the only thirty-something guy that maybe wasn't as straight as he thought he was. He reflected back to their conversation on Saturday night and the feelings of guilt, relief, excitement, and want he'd been processing since. Taking another deep breath, he looked his best friend in the eye to ask the question that had been at the forefront of his mind all week.

"You also said you'd be happy for me to do it again. With you. Is that still true?"

Stu froze in his seat, his glass of wine halfway to his mouth. If the situation hadn't been so serious, Brett would have laughed at the expression of surprise and confusion that flitted across Stu's face. With a blink and a large gulp of wine, Stu set the glass carefully on the coffee table. "You want to kiss me again?" he asked, as if to clarify he'd heard correctly.

"Yeah. I mean, if you don't want to, that's fine. I just thought...well..." Brett's voice tapered off at the closed-off look Stu was giving him. Obviously he'd read the situation wrong and now things would be even more awkward between them. He started to push himself up off the couch. "Yeah. Sorry, mate. Silly idea. I'll...um...see you tomorrow."

"Brett. Stop. Wait." Stuart jumped to his feet and stopped Brett's exit with a hand on his chest. If Stu felt the erratic beating of his heart, he didn't comment on it.

"You took me by surprise. I'm happy for you to kiss me

again, but before we do, I'd like to know why. Where has all this come from? I need to hear it from you without alcohol being involved."

Brett sighed and his shoulders slumped. He knew he had to be honest here otherwise he could screw things up royally.

"Talk to me, B. I doubt there is anything you could say that would shock me. I'm a high school teacher, remember?"

Brett gave a small chuckle at the attempt to lighten the air. Stuart sat back down on the couch, pulling Brett down with him with a tug on his hand. "Now, talk."

"I don't know where to start. One day we're all mates and everything's as it's always been, and then the next I'm having dreams about kissing guys and having thoughts about kissing you."

"Okay. That's fine. There's nothing wrong with that," Stu assured him. "I have that effect on a lot of guys."

Brett gave him a baleful glare. "I'm serious here, Stu. Why am I suddenly having these thoughts? Why, after twenty years, am I suddenly wanting to kiss you?" He could hear the frustration in his voice, and clearly Stu could too, as he laid a calming hand on Brett's arm. Brett tensed up, the muscles in his forearm twitching.

"Relax, idiot. I'm not going to jump you." Stu rolled his eyes. "Just because you've only ever been with women, doesn't mean that this sudden idea of kissing a guy means anything. Your closest friends are all gay and maybe your subconscious has just got curious and is asking, 'what if?' There's no right or wrong reason or answer here, Brett. I know of people that have become curious well into their forties. Just go with it."

Taking a deep breath, Brett consciously worked to relax as he wondered how many of those curious guys Stu had kissed. Stu's voice was low as it broke into his thoughts.

"B, do you want to kiss me again?"

He did want to. He'd tried hard to convince himself that Saturday night had been a one-off, brought on by too much to drink and the relaxing of his inhibitions, but each night as he tried to sleep, the memory of Stu's mouth against his had invaded his dreams, and he'd woken each morning hard and with a yearning to repeat the experience.

"Yeah. I do." Brett admitted as he released a sigh and felt as if a weight had been lifted off his shoulders.

"Well, what are you waiting for?" Stu asked with a grin.

Suddenly he felt shy and inept. This time he didn't have the excuse of being tipsy. He leaned forward, Stu meeting him halfway. Their mouths touched, and Stu gave a small smile before pressing more firmly. Much like their first kiss, this one was tentative, and Brett slowly relaxed. Stu swiped his tongue along the seam of Brett's mouth, and Brett felt a thrill go through him as he let him in. He wanted more and wrapped a hand around Stu's neck, pulling him closer before angling to get a better position

He could taste the wine Stu had gulped down earlier as their tongues stroked together. The rasp of stubble against his thumb had him peppering kisses along Stu's jaw to the soft skin below his ear. Stu let out a soft moan as Brett nibbled his way back to his swollen lips.

He pressed deeper into the kiss and began to push Stu backwards onto the soft couch cushions. He wanted to feel Stu underneath him. Stu's hands grappled at his shoulders as he fought to keep contact with Brett's mouth.

A pained whimper made Brett stop, and he broke away to check Stu was okay.

"Leg," Stu gasped, and Brett realised that Stu's leg was caught beneath them, and as flexible as his friend may be, there was no way he could contort himself backwards while sitting on his own calf. Brett lifted his weight, and Stu managed to straighten himself out, knee narrowly missing Brett's balls in the process.

"Sorry," Stu whispered as he shuffled backwards. Brett shook his head and dipped to capture Stu's mouth again. He really could not get enough of the taste of him. Their chests pressed together and warm hands ran up and down his back, and he arched into the touch.

Below him, Stu shuffled his hips sideways slightly, causing Brett to drop a foot to the floor to avoid falling. A tug at the nape of his neck had him reluctantly pull away from the mouth he was devouring and, not wanting to stop, he again pressed kisses along the softly stubbled jaw, relishing the feel of roughness against his kiss-swollen lips, so different to kissing a girl. He nuzzled under Stu's ear and gave a gentle suck to the soft skin, inhaling the peppermint and lime scent of Stu's bodywash.

Stu gave a slight grunt and his hips twitched before tensing. Brett stopped what he was doing to see Stu's head thrown back with his eyes closed and his lower lip being bitten.

"Are you okay?" Brett asked quietly, his voice husky. Stu's flushed skin darkened further, and when he opened his eyes to look at Brett, his pupils were large and dark.

"Ugh…yeah. More than fine, actually." He gave a small wriggle, and Brett adjusted his weight to allow Stu some breathing room. As he did, he felt the brush of Stu's erection against his thigh. It was his turn to tense and close his eyes. Stu was hard. Because of him. Because of their kiss. A heady rush of exhilaration went through him and his own body responded. He dropped his face back into the crook of Stu's neck, not sure how to react.

A warm hand soothed across his neck and down his spine.

"Are *you* okay?" Stu asked, and Brett could hear the amusement in his voice. He nodded but didn't lift his head, embarrassed. Stu's chest rumbled as he gave a chuckle and he pulled gently on Brett's hair. "B, mate. Look at me."

Brett opened his eyes. Stu gave him a searching glance before pressing a soft kiss to his mouth.

"Don't be embarrassed. You should take it as a compliment. You're a great kisser and it's a natural reaction. For both of us." Stu raised an eyebrow, daring Brett to disagree.

"I...I didn't think that would happen," Brett stammered out. He mentally berated himself. He sounded like a virgin teenager. Of course it was going to happen...wasn't it?

"What is going through your head right now to put that look on your face?" Stu asked him, running his thumb along Brett's cheek. "And what is making you blush like that?" He chuckled as Brett leaned into the touch.

"Umm. This will sound really stupid..."

"B, there are no stupid questions. I've told you; you can talk to me and ask me anything."

Brett huffed a breath. "Okay. Do you normally get...you know...when you kiss a guy?" He nodded in the general direction of their lower bodies.

"What? Are you asking if I usually get hard when a guy kisses me?"

Brett nodded, cringing internally. Could he be any lamer?

"Well, sometimes. It depends on the guy and the circumstances." Stu gave him a questioning look. "Do you get hard every time you kiss a girl?" he countered back.

Brett started to reply but stopped. He hadn't thought of that and now felt even more stupid for asking the question.

"Ah, no. I guess I don't," Brett admitted sheepishly. His mind jumped in the other direction. So, had Stu been genuinely turned on by their kiss. Or was it just because he hadn't been laid in a while? But no, that wasn't right. He'd had that guy over a few weeks ago, when Brett had first moved in. But not since then that he knew of, so for Stu, that qualified as a while.

"Oh my God!"

At Stu's exclamation, Brett was pulled from his thoughts.

"What?" he asked.

"I can smell the burning from here! Stop overthinking it, B." Stu's hands clasped his face, forcing him to look straight at him. "Yes, you turned me on with that kiss. You are a bloody good kisser, and I defy anyone *not* to be turned on when you kiss them like that."

Stu's words sent a burst of happiness through him and, impulsively, he pecked a kiss on the mouth smiling widely at him.

Stu shuffled again, and Brett resisted the urge to hold him in place. He liked the feeling of Stu's body under his. As much as he liked the softness of a woman, the strength in Stu's arms around him and the broad width of his chest was just as much as a turn on. He reluctantly eased himself off, and Stu sat up, not so discreetly adjusting himself as he settled back into the corner of the couch.

He eyed his friend warily. He wasn't sure of the protocol after making out with your best friend. He wondered if he could Google it.

"So, ah…what happens now?" he asked.

"Well, now you've kissed a guy and obviously liked it, do you want to go further?" Stu glanced at his crotch before lifting his gaze back to Brett's, clearly amused. "Do you want to…ah…take things in hand? If you catch my drift?"

Take things in hand? What things…oh. Oh! Brett didn't need a mirror to know he'd turned as red as one of the trucks at work. He could feel his face burning and he looked anywhere but at the other man.

"Well. That answers *that* question," Stu said wryly.

"Wait. No. Stop. Just give me a minute, okay?" Brett raised his hand at his friend. At Stu's nod, Brett took a second to centre himself. Did he want to take things further? He'd been turned on as much as Stu had been, and he couldn't deny the thought of being touched had his dick thickening.

Was he ready for that? Could he return the favour? Could he touch Stu intimately? He wanted to, he knew that much, but the thought made him nervous. The conflict of thoughts and emotions was exhausting, and he didn't know how to respond without hurting Stu.

He glanced at his friend, trying to gauge what Stu was thinking, but only saw patience and quiet understanding on his face.

"You don't have to decide right now. Have a think, and if you decide you want to try more than just kissing, then you know where to find me." Stu gave him a sassy wink and grin as he stood up.

"You…you want to…y'know…with me?" he stammered out.

"Yes, B. I'm happy to be your experiment. Now, stop stressing and go to bed. You've got an early start in the morning."

"Thanks, mate," Brett called out after him as Stu left the room.

"My pleasure, B."

He groaned quietly to himself. Kissing Stu again had not made things easier. It had only opened up more questions. Stu wasn't the only one that had got hard while making out. Was it because he hadn't slept with anyone in almost a year or was it because he was attracted to Stu? He could still feel the tingle on his skin where Stu's stubble had rasped against his and the thought of that roughness scraping against other parts of his body had his dick twitching again.

Brett hauled himself off the couch and moved around the house, shutting off lights and checking locks. He briefly considered a quick shower to cool his overheated body but decided against it. He liked the scent of Stu lingering faintly on his skin; it was something he could get used to.

Chapter Ten

Stu stared unseeing out the classroom window. His best friend and their make-out session a week ago completely occupied his mind. Brett had acted relatively normal since then; their kisses not being discussed by unspoken mutual agreement but there had been lingering glances and brushes of hands when they were close to each other, as if Brett was testing out his feelings and gauging Stu's reactions. Stu had replayed in his mind everything that had happened over the last ten days though. Their friendship had certainly taken a twist, and he wasn't sure what to make of it. He'd more than enjoyed being kissed by Brett, and even days after, his body warmed at the memory, and he had wondered if Brett would take it further. Something Stuart was not averse to following through on.

"Mr Johnson, sir. Do you have a minute?" The sound of Sam Miller's voice broke into his wayward thoughts.

"Hi, Sam. Yes, of course I do. What can I help you with?" Stu smiled at the seventeen-year-old and got a less than bright one in return.

Sam glanced over his shoulder at the door before pushing it almost closed. Stu waved to a chair next to his desk. Clearly, there was something on Sam's mind.

"Is everything okay, Sam?"

"Um...yeah. I just wanted…wanted to ask…um…" A fiery blush coloured Sam's face and he stared down at his feet, his hands twisting nervously in his lap. Stu frowned. This was not usual behaviour for the naturally confident teen.

"Sam. Whatever it is, you can tell me in total confidence, okay?" Stu said reassuringly.

Sam inhaled deeply and looked up. "I'm gay," he announced in a rush of breath before dropping his gaze again.

Stu tried hard not to visibly react. It was not what he'd expected Sam to say, and he knew from experience that any reaction to coming out could have an impact on how Sam behaved in the future

"Okay. That's fine. Am I the first person you've come out to?" he asked gently.

Sam shook his head. "I…I told my mum and dad over the holidays."

"How did they take it?" Stu was nervous about Sam's response. There were some parents out there that did not take kindly to a child coming out.

"They were surprised, and I think they're okay with it. They haven't said a lot, but they both hugged me."

"That's a great start." Stuart gave what he hoped was a reassuring smile. "How do you feel about being gay?"

Sam's head shot up in surprise. "I…I…don't know." He gave a small shrug. "I s'pose I'm scared and confused and…and…" His voice tailed off and he dropped his gaze again.

"Those are all natural feelings, Sam. Why don't we start with what scares you the most?"

"I guess what people will say when they find out." Tears shimmered in his eyes, and Stuart felt for the young man. He could understand Sam's fears. Being a popular, bright seventeen-year-old, he would be worried about what his peers would say. Even though Stu was comfortable in his own skin now and really didn't give a shit what anyone thought about him, when he had come out nearly twenty years ago, society hadn't been as accepting and he had lost a few supposed friends in the process. The one person who had stuck by him was Brett.

He leaned forward on the desk and spoke softly. "Sam, I'm going to be honest with you and I'm not going to sugar coat it. There will be some people who it won't matter to, and there will be people who will never talk to you again." He gave a small chuckle. "You are lucky that being gay doesn't quite have the stigma today as it did when I came out. The thing you have to remember is that you are true to yourself and, yes, it will hurt and you will have things said to you that are not nice, but there will always be those in your life that love you regardless of who you love."

Sam gave a small nod. "Mum and Dad said that. They said I will have to be careful of who I tell and that maybe I should reconsider what I want to do when I leave school."

"They have some valid points, but what do they mean about after you leave school?" Stu was a little confused by the comment. Being gay shouldn't stop Sam from pursuing whatever career he wanted to.

"Well, the plan was for me to do a building apprenticeship. I don't want to go to university. I prefer working with my hands, and Mr Collier says he knows a few guys that would take me on as an apprentice, but now I've told my dad I'm gay, he thinks it will be harder for me to get a job in that industry." The disappointment in Sam's voice was clear.

"I'm sure your dad means well, and I know that Mr Collier has sung your praises more than once in the staff room, but being gay doesn't mean that you can't be a builder. In fact, one of my closest friends is a builder with his own successful company and he's got a boyfriend, so it's not impossible."

"Really?" Hope flared in Sam's face, and Stuart could see some of the tension ease from his shoulders.

"Yes, really. I can arrange a meeting with him for you if you like. You can have a chat about what things he's faced in the industry. I even think he's looking for some extra hands for a big renovation job he's doing at the moment. I can ask him to take you on for some work experience if you want."

"That would be awesome, sir," Sam said excitedly.

"I'll ring him tonight and then, if he's okay with it, we'll organise a time to meet and I'll email your parents and get their permission," Stu told him, smiling as he did. "Now, are there any other questions you have? Do I need to give you the safe sex lecture?"

"Ugh, no. Definitely not. I had it twice from Mum and Dad separately, and besides, I'm not at that stage yet," Sam said with a roll of his eyes, a faint blush staining his cheeks.

"Fair enough, I'll let you off. Remember though, there are people here at school, as well as myself, that can help you out if you have questions."

"Thanks, sir. I think I'll be okay." Sam stood and hiked his backpack onto his shoulder. He was back to being the happy kid that Stu knew.

A knock at the door had them both looking up. Sam's best friend, Jack Lewis, was standing there.

"There you are. I've been looking everywhere for you." His glance flicked between his friend and Stuart. Concern creased his brow. "Everything all right, mate?" he asked.

Sam looked at Stuart, who shrugged. It was up to Sam who and when he told people.

"Yeah. I…um…need to tell you something."

Jack stepped further into the room, his bag sliding down his arm. "What? What's happened. Are you all right?"

Stu was pleased to see the genuine concern Jack had for Sam.

"I…I…I'm gay, Jack," Sam stammered out, watching his best friend carefully.

"Okay. Has someone said something to you? 'Cos you know if they have, I'll be having words with them," Jack said vehemently.

"What? No, no one has said anything." Sam was surprised at his friend's response. Stuart smiled to himself. Jack's reaction was very similar to how Brett had reacted when he'd come out to him when they were teens.

"Did you hear what I said, Jack? I told you I'm gay."

"Yeah. So? Just because you're into guys doesn't mean you aren't still crap at *Fortnite*," Jack replied with a shrug.

"I'm not crap at *Fortnite*," Sam shot back.

"Yeah, mate, you are. You die, in like, five minutes of landing on the island."

"Bullshit. I—"

Stu decided it was time to step in. "Boys, I don't know about you, but I'd like to go home sometime today. Can you continue this discussion elsewhere?"

"Oh, yeah. Sorry, sir." Sam gave him a sheepish smile. "Thanks for the advice. And you'll let me know what your friend says?"

"Yes. I'll talk to you tomorrow."

Stuart watched as the two friends left the room, noting how Jack threw his arm over Sam's shoulders while still arguing he was the better video game player. He smiled to himself. He was happy that Sam was comfortable enough to feel he could talk to him and come out to him. It had been a lot harder for him when he'd been that age.

He remembered coming out to Brett all those years ago. His friend's reaction at the time had done a lot for his confidence, and Brett had become one of his fiercest protectors when some of the guys on their soccer team had found out. They'd pointed the finger at Brett too, accusing him of being Stu's boyfriend, but Brett hadn't backed down, and it hadn't taken long for them to realise that their hate was being ignored.

Stu was glad that Sam's parents seemed accepting and had offered some support. It would be an adjustment for them all, but it looked like they were heading in the right direction. His parents had not expressed much of an opinion either way. They'd just told him to stay safe and then asked how'd he'd done on his English test.

As he drove home, he mused whether Brett would decide to take things further between them and if he did, would he decide he was bi, and would he come out? Stu knew their friends wouldn't care that Brett was exploring his sexuality. Admittedly they'd tease him mercilessly, but it would be harmless and in fun.

Being able to freely run his hands through Brett's hair the other night had reignited old memories and dreams. He'd never told anyone how he felt about Brett and over the years he'd outgrown his teenage crush, or at least he thought he had. He couldn't let feelings get involved. It would cause too much heartbreak all round.

*****

Tipping his head into the stream of hot water, Brett groaned softly as tension eased from his shoulders and back. Although he was used to hard work, the muscles he'd used the last few days working with Charlie on the renovation of Cooper's house ached. The reno was a big job, with the whole house being gutted back to its original framing and being rebuilt with new everything. Brett had again stayed out in one of the cottages on the property next door that belonged to Charlie's siblings. It was easier than commuting nearly an hour each way every day.

He'd messaged Stu several times over the last few days, not wanting the other man to think he was ghosting him again. Despite enjoying his time with Charlie and Cooper, he'd found himself wanting to be at home with Stu, but he'd promised to help Charlie out and the extra money was always good.

The lingering scent of Stu's body wash in the air had his body tightening with a different tension as the memory of feeling Stu's lithe body under his and the taste of Stu surfaced. Not for the first time since last week, his dick began to fill, and Brett stroked himself slowly to the memories of kissing Stu again invading his brain. These soon branched out into fantasies of them doing more than just kissing. He wanted to see Stu lose control, and the idea had his hand speeding up, and within moments his release barrelled through him.

Leaning against the tiled wall, he caught his breath before quickly washing himself off. It was no use pretending that a few kisses were enough. He wanted to try more, and he only hoped Stu's offer was still open.

Fifteen minutes later, he wandered into the kitchen to find his best friend laughing while on his cell phone. Stu gave him a wave of acknowledgement as he continued his conversation, and Brett took the opportunity to look him over. He no longer looked at Stu as just a mate, now noticing small things like how his dirty blond hair was slightly tousled, as if he'd been running his hand through it. He'd never appreciated how Stu's whole face lit up when he was genuinely amused, light sparkling in his blue eyes, and his gaze drifted down to the wide mouth with lips that were firm yet silky soft at the same time and had felt so good against his own.

Stu had obviously not been home long as he was still in his work clothes of dress pants and pale blue button-down that clung to his broad shoulders before tapering to a narrow waist. As he watched, Stu turned slightly and leaned against the kitchen counter, concentrating on whatever the person on the other end of the phone was saying, hip popping out. Brett's fingers twitched with the urge to run over the tight swell of buttocks showcased by the dark navy material.

Stu looked up and caught his eye and frowned slightly in question. Something must have shown on his face because Stu started to wrap up his call.

"Thanks, Charlie. I really appreciate it. I'll check with Sam tomorrow when his study leave starts, and we can arrange a time for him to come out and have a chat." Stu nodded. "Yeah, you too. See you later. Bye."

Stu put down his phone and leaned back against the counter, giving a bright smile that caused all sorts of flutters in Brett's chest. "Hey, stranger. How are you?"

Brett didn't reply. He took two strides until he was in front of Stuart.

"B, you okay?" Stu asked him, smile fading slightly at the sudden movement.

Brett drank in the familiar features that he'd missed seeing before cupping Stu's jaw in his left hand, lowering his head, and kissing him. Stu gave a small yelp of surprise, and Brett took advantage of the parted lips to slip his tongue into the warm recesses of Stu's mouth. It only took a second or two before Stu was returning the kiss, his arms wrapping around Brett's waist to pull him closer as they hungrily ate at each other.

Pushing Stu against the counter to steady them, Brett deepened the kiss. He couldn't get enough of this. He'd missed seeing Stu the last few days and any doubts he'd had about wanting to do more, learn more, went out the window.

"B, mate. Stop," Stu gasped out as he pulled his mouth away.

Brett froze, ice dashing through his veins as he relaxed his grip on Stu and moved back.

Stu's hand tightened on his waist, stilling him. "No, it's okay. I just need a second."

Brett paused, taking in the questioning look his friend was giving him. "Sorry…" he started to say before Stu placed a finger on his lips, halting him.

"No, don't apologise. I wasn't expecting you to…"

"Maul you?"

Stu grinned. "Well, that's one way to put it. I'm not complaining, just surprised. I…ah…take it you're comfortable kissing a guy now?"

"What gave it away?" Brett teased, slipping back into the easy banter that had been the cornerstone of their twenty-year friendship.

"Oh, I don't know. Maybe your tongue in my mouth, or the fact you pinned me against the bench without even saying hello," Stu retorted with a quirk of his eyebrow.

Brett gave into temptation and pressed a kiss to the grinning mouth. "Hi, how was your day?" he asked, his voice low.

Stu returned the kiss with a chuckle and wound his arms around Brett's neck. "So what brought that on?"

"I…ah…was going to talk to you later. But then I saw you there looking so damn sexy in those clothes, and all I could think about was kissing you again and how much I want…" Brett trailed off, uncertainty washing through him.

"How much you want, what?" Stu asked, softly running a hand through the hair at his nape.

"Ah…to…um…*maybedomorethankissing.*" Brett rushed out, suddenly feeling vulnerable.

"What kind of things?"

"T-t-touching," Brett whispered. His heart was beating like a drum and he felt all kinds of embarrassed and strangely turned on all at the same time. He watched Stu's face carefully, waiting for any sign of ridicule or worse, rejection.

Stu slid his fingers around his neck, coming to rest at the base of his throat. "This kind of touching?" he asked.

Brett shook his head, and Stu smirked before trailing his fingers down his chest, tips resting on his pec. Brett couldn't help the involuntarily gasp as his nipple pebbled under his thin t-shirt. Stu's fingers gently brushed against the hardened nub. "This kind of touching?" he rasped, his voice low.

Brett nodded, licks of fire coursing through him as Stu leaned in closer. Brett could smell the faint trace of his cologne and wanted to bury his face in Stu's neck and absorb everything he could. He shivered as Stu's hand slipped further down, coming to rest on his waist. Unable to take much more, Brett slid his hands around Stu's slim hips and gave into the temptation to run them over the tight butt he'd been admiring earlier.

"I want you to touch me all over," he murmured as he gently squeezed, and it was Stu's turn to gasp and bury his face in Brett's neck. "And touch you too."

"Are you sure?" Warm breath fanned across his heated skin.

"Yes. If…if you are?"

A kiss was pressed against the underside of his jaw before Stuart moved back to look him in the eye.

"I said I would, and I will. But we need to talk first."

Brett groaned and tugged Stu closer, peppering kisses along his throat. He didn't want to talk; he wanted to kiss and touch and explore.

Stu let him nibble at his neck for a moment before pulling away. Brett pouted, and Stu chuckled and kissed him briefly before moving out of his arms.

"I promise, we will do this, B. But we have to set some ground rules. Let me get changed and then we can pick up where we left off." With a quick wink and a grin, Stu headed to his room.

Chapter Eleven

Stuart gently closed his bedroom door and dropped onto his bed, startling a slumbering Bucky and Cap. The cats eyed him briefly and then ignored him. His heart was still racing after that welcome home kiss. It was the last thing he'd expected, and he touched a hand to his slightly swollen mouth. Brett had certainly got over any reservations he had about kissing a guy and now he'd said he wanted to go further. When he'd told Brett he was happy to help him explore his curiosity, he'd expected it to be no more than a couple of kisses, just the fulfilment of an old fantasy He wasn't averse to the idea of going further, Brett was an attractive man after all, but now that Brett wanted to do more, Stu was having conflicting thoughts.

Could they remain friends if they were intimate? If he stopped now, would Brett find someone else to experiment with? A sick feeling rolled through his stomach at that thought. He scrubbed a hand over his face, huffing out a breath. Cap sniffed at his face, and he scratched the purring cat behind his ear.

"What am I going to do, Cap? I don't want to lose B out of my life. What if we do this and then he freaks out again?"

Cap had no advice for him, just a head nudge and a louder purr.

"Ugh! But what happens if he *doesn't* freak out? But what do we do when he decides he's had enough? Things will never be the same again between us, either way, will they? See, this is why I don't do relationships. Too much thinking." He groaned.

Deciding that arguing with himself was getting him nowhere, he forced himself to move and get changed out of his work clothes. He pulled on his favourite pair of sweatpants and t-shirt, taking comfort in the soft material.

He found his best friend slouched on the couch, the TV playing the evening news. Despite his posture, there was tension in Brett's shoulders, his face a blank mask.

Taking his usual spot at the opposite end of the couch, Stu marshalled his thoughts. The only way this could work would be if they were honest with each other.

"So, first things first," Stuart started. "Are you absolutely sure about this?"

"Yes. If by 'this', you mean going further than kissing, then yes, I am," Brett told him, his voice firm and confident.

"Okay. How far do you want to go?"

Brett dropped his gaze and traced a pattern on his leg, not responding immediately. Stuart gently prompted him, "You mentioned touching earlier." Brett nodded, and he continued. "What kind of touching? Are we talking hand jobs, sucking…fucking?" That got a response as Brett paled slightly and wide eyes lifted to meet Stu's.

"I…ah…I don't know?" he stammered.

"Okay. We'll come back to that," Stu said, not wanting to push his friend into anything he didn't want to do. He looked Brett in the eye. "More importantly, in fact, the most important thing of all, is that I will not do this with you if it is going to fuck up our friendship." Brett opened his mouth to speak, but Stuart held a hand up. "Wait a sec, let me say this and you can have your turn." Brett nodded and settled further into the corner of the couch.

"Your friendship means more to me than anything else in this world, Brett. I will not jeopardise that just because you've got curious, okay? You have to promise me that this will not make things weird between us, regardless of how it turns out."

"It won't, I promise," Brett butted in.

"Really? You freaked out and disappeared for days after we kissed that first time. I mean it, B. You need to be one hundred percent certain that this is what you want, because I will not throw away twenty years over a few kisses and a blowjob." Stu warned him.

Brett nodded in agreement. "You're right. Our friendship is the most important thing here. I know I can say I won't freak out again, but to be honest, I really don't know if I will or not."

"Okay. Fair enough. So, we've established you're okay with kissing. Next step is touching. You said you want me to touch you all over?"

"Yeah, I do," Brett admitted shyly.

"I presume you want an orgasm or two in there somewhere?" Stu couldn't help but ask with a grin.

Brett gave a choked cough and a dull stain rose under his skin, but he managed to grin back. "Yeah. That would be good."

Relaxing into the arm of the couch, Stu decided to see how far Brett would go. "So, frotting and hand jobs are good? What about sucking? Could you cope with a blowjob?"

"Mate. I'm a bloke. What guy doesn't like a blowjob?" Brett taunted with a raised eyebrow.

"I've met one or two in my time, believe me. However, that is not a story for now, or ever actually." Stu dismissed the comment with a wave of his hand. "What I mean is, could you cope having a blowjob from a guy? And could you see yourself returning the favour?"

"Ah…um…" Brett spluttered, his face going even redder.

"It's all well and good to say you want to go further than kissing, B, but it can't be all one sided," Stu told him gently. He wasn't trying to be unkind, and he knew he'd get pleasure out of it, but he had to know for sure that Brett was going to be a willing participant in all of this.

Brett sat up straighter and gave him a sincere look. "Yes. Yes, I could cope having a guy sucking me off, and I think I could return the favour."

"The next most important thing, is that at any point you want to stop, if at any time you feel uncomfortable, you say so." Consent was important to Stu, even more so in this case.

"Stu, I trust you. I know you wouldn't force me to do something I'm not comfortable with. That's why I wanted to do this with you and haven't just gone out to find some random guy to try this with. And it works both ways, mate. If you don't want to do something, you have to tell me as well. I want this to be good for you too."

Stu's eyes pricked at Brett's words, and he closed them and took a deep breath to get himself under control. Brett's thoughtfulness and compassion were just two of the things Stu admired in him. It was part of the reason he was so good at his job.

The idea of Brett doing any of this with someone other than him didn't help either. It just added to the mess of thoughts swirling through his brain.

"What about fucking?" he blurted out, not wanting Brett to pick up on his other emotions.

"I don't think so," Brett said, his gaze dropping. "I can't picture myself do...doing that," he rushed out before glancing briefly back at Stu. "Is that a deal breaker for you?"

"What? No. Definitely not. If you don't want to do anal, then that's fine. It's not unusual for some guys not to have full penetrative sex," Stu rushed to reassure him.

"Really? What about you? You like it, though?"

"I generally top. I mean, I have bottomed, but I don't really enjoy it, so I don't," Stu replied honestly. There was no point hiding his preferences.

"Are you sure? I don't want you to feel cheated because I won't let you fuck me."

Stu shook his head. "That works both ways, you know. Will you feel cheated if I don't let you fuck me? Besides, if you feel you want to later on, then we can talk about it again."

Brett didn't reply, and Stu decided they'd talked enough for now. He stood and reached out a hand.

"Come on. I think we've covered enough of the basics for now. Let's just take this one step at a time, okay?"

*****

Brett stared at the hand Stu was holding out to him. What he'd said was true. He did trust Stuart, and although he'd claimed he could find someone else to do this with, he really couldn't imagine doing it with anyone else. His stomach churned with what felt like a kaleidoscope of butterflies and his hands were clammy.

Rubbing his palms down his thighs, he took the offered hand and let Stu haul him to his feet. He got an encouraging grin before Stu led him down the hallway to his room.

Brett paused just inside the doorway, his heart racing and his mouth dry. He didn't think he'd been this nervous when he'd lost his virginity at sixteen. He tracked Stu's movements around the room as he flicked on one of the bedside lamps before shooing the cats out and pulling the covers back on the bed.

"You okay?" Stu asked as he came back to stand in front of him.

Brett nodded and, gathering his wits about him, walked further into the room. Stu gave him a smile before leaning past him to push the door closed. The click of the main light switch being flicked off sounded loudly before everything was bathed in the warm, muted glow of the bedside lamp.

Firm lips pressed against his throat as Stu stepped closer into his body. "Relax, B. This is your show. Just do what feels comfortable, okay?"

"O-okay." Resting his palms on Stu's hips, he caught Stu's mouth in a kiss, taking his time to savour the taste as his thumbs sought out the soft skin above the waistband of the sweatpants his best friend wore.

Warm hands slid around his neck before strong fingers were threading through his hair, pulling slightly. A tendril of desire snaked down his spine to settle low in his groin, and he tugged Stu as close as he could. Another jolt of heat went through him as he felt an answering hardness press against his thigh.

A small moan escaped him as Stu pulled his mouth away. "This will be more comfortable on the bed," Stu told him, and Brett let himself be led the short distance across the room. A tug on the hem of his t-shirt had him raising his arms, allowing it to be pulled over his head. Once his shirt was off, Stu removed his own and then moved onto the bed.

Brett took in the sight before him. The light from the lamp highlighted the dips and curves of Stu's chest and abs. He wasn't as chiselled as Brett was, but there was some definition there, along with a smattering of fine blond hairs. His gaze dropped further to the tented sweatpants. His skin heated with a blush as he quickly averted his eyes only to find Stu watching him with a small smile.

"Come here," Stu said, reaching out his hand.

Brett climbed onto the bed, the mattress dipping under his weight as he slid down so they were face to face. Goosebumps raced along his skin as Stu gently ran a hand down his shoulder and across his chest. Like he had earlier in the kitchen, he paused at Brett's pec before caressing it with this thumb. The small nub hardened, and a rush of blood headed south.

Warm lips travelled down his throat, over his collarbone, before dipping to flick at his nipple, and Brett couldn't stop the groan that escaped him as he arched his back in response. He'd never realised how sensitive his nipples were and his hand slipped behind Stu's head to gently hold him in place as the other man licked and suckled at his skin.

Slowly and torturously, Stu moved down his body. When he reached the waistband of Brett's jeans, he paused, tapping against the button as he looked up at Brett.

"We still good?" he asked, his voice husky.

"Yeah," Brett huffed out, his hips jerking up of their own accord. Stu gave him a grin before straddling his thighs and popping the metal disc undone. Without breaking eye contact, his nimble fingers slowly drew the zipper down, and Brett felt relief as his cock was freed from the confines of the denim.

He gave a small yelp when Stu ran his hand along his dick. At the questioning look he got, he nodded. "I'm good. Please…"

"Please…what?" Stu asked, a sly smile spreading across his face.

"Touch me. Please." He thrust his hips up, trying to get more pressure and friction.

"Like this, you mean?" Stu teased as he trailed his fingers lightly down the straining shaft. "Or do you mean like this?" Firmer pressure was applied, causing Brett to groan and push towards Stu.

With a chuckle, Stu tugged at Brett's jeans and underwear, quickly removing them. "You need to strip too," Brett told him. He was feeling a little vulnerable, lying there naked on the bed as Stu's eyes roved over him. His dick jerked as Stu licked his lips, face raw with desire as he stripped out of his sweatpants, and Brett got a brief glimpse of Stu's cock before the other man was plastered on top of him, mouth greedily kissing his.

Brett wrapped his arms around Stu and opened his thighs, allowing Stu to settle between them, groin to groin. He had a second to marvel at the strength in Stu's torso before his hips began to rock, and Brett gasped at the sensation of hard flesh rubbing against his own. Everything was so different, but at the same time, so right. Stu slid a hand between them and began to firmly stroke Brett's aching shaft. The sensation of Stu's hand wrapping around him had him moaning loudly, thrusting into the tight grasp. Stu swiped his thumb over the leaking head, using the pre-come to lubricate the glide of his fist.

Without conscious thought, his own hand reached down and wrapped around Stu's hardness. A vague thought flitted through his brain at the fact he had another guy's dick in his grip but quickly disappeared when Stu grunted and rocked his hips.

"Fuck, B. That feels so good." Warmth spread through Brett at Stu's whispered praise. He'd always got pleasure from making his partner feel good. A burst of pre-come slicked against his fingers and, tightening his grip on Stu, he increased the pace of his strokes. "Ungh. Shit." Stu's whimpers had Brett pulling him closer, thrusting his tongue into the warm cavern of Stu's mouth.

Suddenly, Stu launched himself away from Brett, slipping out of his grasp.

"Where are you going? What's wrong?" Brett asked, confused. Stu couldn't be having second thoughts now. "Did I...did I do something wrong?"

Chest heaving, Stu shook his head. "No. Definitely not. In fact, you are doing everything right. I just need a second. I want this to be about you, and at the rate we're going, I'll be done before you." Stu leaned over to press a soft kiss to Brett's mouth before shimmying down the bed to lie between Brett's thighs.

"What are you doing down there?" Brett asked, even though he had a good idea of what was coming next.

"This." A wicked grin crossed Stu's face before he licked a stripe from the base of Brett's cock to the tip. Sensation raced through Brett and he gripped the sheets.

"Okay?" Stu checked with him. Brett nodded and dropped back onto the pillow as Stu chuckled and repeated the action before sucking the sensitive head into his mouth.

"Oh, fuck!" Brett's strangled cursed echoed around the room. The warm, wet heat of Stu's mouth enveloped him, and although he didn't think it was possible, his dick hardened more. His hips gave an involuntary lurch as he chased after Stu's talented tongue. He couldn't remember the last time he'd had a blowjob, but he could remember that it had never felt like this. There was nothing tentative about the way Stu was using his mouth and hands to tease him. Lou had rarely given him head and when she did, it had been soft and gentle. This was everything but, and Brett could do nothing but lose himself in the sensation of it all.

He grunted as his heavy balls were gently squeezed and a finger firmly rubbed at the sensitive skin below. A tingling in his spine had him grasping towards Stu, fingers slipping into the soft blond hair. "Stu, mate. I'm cl-close. Argh. Fuck."

Stu gave him one last suck before pulling off and crawling up the bed to kiss him. Brett's tongue met Stu's and he could taste the faint muskiness of himself. Pushing gently on Stu's shoulders, he rolled on top of him, lips never breaking contact. He couldn't get enough of this. He ground his hips into Stu's, setting a steady rhythm.

Stu's right leg hooked across his hip and he arched up into Brett. "Right there, B. Don't stop."

"Couldn't if I wanted t-to," Brett panted out, his face buried in Stu's warm neck. He lifted up on his elbows to gain more leverage, his only focus now the growing heat in his groin. The sensitive head of his cock rubbed against Stu's matching hard length. He glanced down and the sight of them together had him speeding up his thrusts.

"Oh…oh…I'm…yes…" Whimpers escaped him as his balls tightened and he erupted with a shout. He dropped his head next to Stu's, mouthing at the sweat-slicked skin of Stu's throat as he continued to rut, dragging out his orgasm as long as he could. Stu tensed below him, hands gripping at his hips, pulling him impossibly closer, and then he was coming with his own loud groan.

Their frantic movements gradually slowed as they caught their breaths. Brett kept his face buried in the pillow, trying to catch his breath. A gentle caress on his back had him snuggling closer into Stu's side. He didn't want to move. Not because he was embarrassed, but because it all felt right. He wasn't having an epiphany that this was what had been missing all his adult life, but he felt like a piece of a puzzle had slotted into place, and it felt good. And right.

"You okay, B?" Stu asked him, his voice barely above a whisper. Brett hummed before pressing a kiss under Stu's ear. "You ever going to look at me again, or are you going to hide in that pillow for the rest of your life?"

"I'm never going to look at you the same way again," Brett mumbled. Stuart tensed, and Brett replayed the words in his head, realisation dawning. He pushed up on his elbows to peer into his best friend. "No. I didn't mean it that way. What I meant was…"

"No, it's okay. You don't have to explain," Stu interrupted and began to push Brett off him.

"Oi. Stop." Brett grappled at Stu's torso as he tried to move out from under him. He put a hand on Stu's face, holding him in place as he forced Stu to look at him. "I thought freaking out was my job, not yours? I promise you: I enjoyed every single second of what we just did. And what I meant when I said I'm not going to look at you the same way again, was that I will now be imaging you naked. And hard. And under me." He punctuated each statement with a kiss.

He quirked an eyebrow, daring the other man to argue. Stu's mouth twitched as he fought not to grin. "So, are we okay? he asked. Stu lifted his head to meet Brett's mouth. The kiss was languorous and sensual, and Brett's dick gave a half-hearted twitch.

Stu chuckled and pulled away. "There are some wank wipes in the drawer on your side."

"Prepared much?" Brett teased.

"Easier than wandering down the hall for a cloth to clean up with. Nicer than tissues."

At Stu's explanation, Brett became conscious of how sticky things were between them and gave a slightly disgusted groan. "Ugh."

"Yeah, it's a bit messier than what you're used to, I should imagine."

"Hmm. Yeah. Didn't really think of that," Brett told him as he rolled over and pulled open the top drawer of the cabinet. He pulled out the packet of wipes and removed three or four. He waved Stu's hand away as he reached for them and gently cleaned him. He smirked when Stu's spent cock gave a twitch at the ministrations. He quickly wiped himself down and wadded the dirty wipes into a ball before dropping them into the small rubbish bin next to the bed.

"Thanks," Stu murmured sleepily. "So, what happens now, B?"

"Well, seeing as we both have work tomorrow, I suggest sleep." He snuggled into Stu's side.

"Comfortable?"

Brett's post-orgasm glow quickly disappeared at the dry tone. "Oh. Yeah. Sorry, not used to this. I'll…um…head back to my room then. Let you get some sleep. I'm…um…back on shift tomorrow…so, yeah…I'll catch you later." He kicked away the covers and scrambled to roll out of the bed. Stu's hand on his arm prevented him from getting far.

"Stop, you idiot. I meant, what happens now we've done this little experiment? Do you want to do it again?"

Brett leaned against the headboard and tugged the sheet back over his waist. Stu sat up and did the same. "Yes. I want to do it again. I want to do more."

He risked a glance at Stu, afraid of what he'd see. The shit-eating grin spreading across the familiar features was not what he expected. Brett rolled his eyes. "Oh, for fuck's sake!"

"Told you you'd like it if you tried it," Stu said in a self-satisfied tone.

"You are going to be insufferable now, aren't you?" Brett huffed out, feigning annoyance but secretly relieved they were teasing each other like normal.

"No more than usual, B. No more than usual."

Brett pushed at Stu's shoulder. "Go to sleep, you arsehole. I'll see you in the morning." He climbed out of the bed.

"Hey, Brett?" Stu's voice was quiet and serious, no hint of amusement in his tone.

Brett looked up from picking his clothes up off the floor. "Yeah?"

"You sure you're okay. Sure that we're okay?"

Brett was surprised at the look of vulnerability in Stu's eyes. It was something he hadn't seen in years, not since they were in their teens and Stu had come out to him. The urge to comfort had him reaching across the bed and to brush his mouth against Stu's.

"Yeah, we're good." Another brush of lips. "Thank you."

Before Stu could say any more, Brett winked at him and left the room.

Chapter Twelve

"Wow! What an amazing view," Sam's delighted cry had Stu grinning as he negotiated a large pothole in the gravel driveway leading to Cooper's house. As promised, he was bringing the teen out to meet Charlie. Stu hadn't told him about Cooper and was expecting an excited response when Sam found out whose home they were visiting.

"Yeah, Charlie lives next door. His parents own the bed-and-breakfast lodge and Charlie's got a small cottage at the edge of the property. This one, though, belongs to his boyfriend."

"So he really has a boyfriend? And he's a builder?" Sam asked. Stu could hear the curiosity and uncertainty in his voice.

"Yep. Don't worry, Sam. Charlie will answer any questions you have."

Stu parked and they made their way to the front door. Music was playing in the background and the sounds of hammering and a band saw screeching filled the air. Stu had messaged Charlie to say they were coming, and he carefully entered the house through the open door.

"Charlie!" he yelled as they paused in the foyer. Although nowhere near finished, the bare bones of a light and open space greeted them. A curving staircase was to their right, the pale wooden bannister covered in protective plastic.

"Through here, Stu," Charlie's deep baritone echoed from the back of the house. Stu nodded to Sam and led them through a doorway. A grinning Charlie greeted them as they entered the large open-plan area. He was wiping his hands on an old towel as he crossed over to them.

"How are you, Stu?" Charlie asked as he pulled him into a bro-hug.

"Yeah, good, thanks. You?"

"Never better." Charlie grinned and stuck his hand out to Sam. "You must be Sam. Nice to meet you."

"Thanks for letting me come out to see you, Mr Samuels," Sam replied as he confidently shook Charlie's hand.

"Agh, none of that 'Mr Samuels' stuff. Call me Charlie." Stu saw Sam's shoulders relax slightly as he nodded at Charlie's request.

"Stu here tells me you're keen on becoming a builder. Have you had any experience in the industry?"

Sam began telling Charlie about his part-time job at the local hardware store and some of the projects he'd worked on with his dad at home. Soon they were looking through photos on Sam's phone and Charlie was showing him the plans for the renovation and pointing out what had been done so far.

Left to his own devices while they talked, Stu's mind began to wander over the last couple of weeks. Brett had kept his promise of not freaking out, and they had experimented some more, with lots of kissing and making out on the couch in the evenings, frotting sessions, and a blowjob that had left Brett almost comatose. Stu was still chuckling about that. Once he'd regained his faculties, Brett had finally admitted that maybe Stu and the guys were right and that a guy could come so hard he'd forget his name.

Whilst he was enjoying the new turn in their friendship, he was still worried how things were going to go once it ran its course. His emotions ran from one end of the scale to the other, from anticipation and excitement to stress and nerves. He was doing his best to not let Brett see the darker emotions, not wanting to cast a shadow on their friendship.

"Stu, mate. You with us?" Charlie's amused voice broke into his thoughts.

"What? Sorry, Charlie. I was miles away."

"I know. I could see that," Charlie said with a chuckle. "Anyway, I was saying to Sam that if it's okay with his parents, he can come and get some work experience here with me. Is there anything I need to do to make it official with the school?"

"I'm not sure. I can check when we get back and let you know." Stu looked at Sam, excitement making his face glow. "You're keen then, Sam? How are you going to get out here and back?" he asked. It was a good forty-minute drive out to the property.

"I've suggested he come and stay over at Mum's. She's got a spare room. Sam just has to get permission from his parents."

"I've got my restricted licence too, Mr Johnson, and I've almost got enough saved to buy a car. Dad and I are going to look at some over the weekend."

"Okay then. We can talk to the school and your parents and work things out." Stu smiled at Charlie. "Thanks, Charlie. I really appreciate it."

"Hey, it's a win-win for both of us. Sam gets some valuable work experience, and I get someone that actually knows one end of a hammer from another." Charlie's grin was bright, his eyes dancing with amusement. "Besides, he can't be any worse than the apprentice I've currently got," he said with a wink.

"Hey! I'm not that bad," a distinctly English voice said from behind them.

Stu and Charlie laughed at the indignant tone and turned to see Cooper walking in with a tray of coffee mugs.

"No, babe, you're not. Your coffee making skills are out of this world," Charlie retorted as he took the proffered mug from his boyfriend. At Cooper's disgruntled snort, Charlie kissed him on the cheek and waved at Sam.

"Cooper, this is Sam. He's going to come and give us a hand and get some work experience while he's at it."

"Hi, Sam, good to meet you," Cooper said, giving a megawatt smile to the gaping teenager before turning to Stu. "Stu, how are ya?" he asked as he pulled him forward into a hug.

"Good thanks, Coop. You're looking more awake than the last time I saw you," Stu teased before noticing that Sam was looking at them, bewildered.

"Sam, this is Cooper Evans. If you hadn't guessed, he's Charlie's boyfriend and the owner of this place."

"You…I…It's a pleasure to meet you, sir." Sam said shyly.

"Oh Christ, Sam. Don't call him 'sir'. I'll never hear the end of it," Charlie rolled his eyes with a grin.

Recognising the look in Cooper's eyes as he opened his mouth to retort, Stu jumped in. "Okay, guys. Please don't traumatise my student any more than you have to, hmmm?"

"Sorry, Sam. Now, come over here and let me tell you what it's really like working for Charlie," Cooper said as he slung an arm over Sam's shoulders.

"Don't believe a word he says, Sam," Charlie called out, getting a laugh in response.

"Things good between you then?" Stu asked as he sipped his coffee.

"Yeah. Never thought I could be this happy," Charlie admitted softly as he watched Sam laugh at something Cooper had said. "How about you, Stu? Things okay with you?"

Confused at the questioning gaze Charlie was giving him, he asked, "Of course. Why?"

"No reason. Just checking in. Is it going okay have Brett staying with you? I know you like your own space."

"Actually, it's going better than I thought. I hardly see him, you know, with his shifts and then him coming out here to work with you. No problems at all. Really good. Yeah." Stu nodded.

"That's good. Is there anything going on with Brett?"

Stu choked on the mouthful of coffee he'd just swallowed. After a small coughing fit and Charlie patting him on the back, he managed to reply. "Not that I know of. Why'd you ask?"

"Nothing in particular. He's been a bit off the last few times he's been over, and then this last week, he seemed a lot more relaxed. Just wondered if there was something going on with him."

"Dunno. If there is, he hasn't said anything to me," Stu lied, hoping like hell his face wasn't giving him away. It was up to Brett if he wanted to tell their friends about their relationship. *Relationship?* Where had that thought come from? Stu didn't do relationships. This was just a bit of fun with a friend. *Wasn't it?* Stu tamped down the panic he could feel rising in his chest.

Thankfully he was saved from saying any more as Cooper and Sam joined them. Stu looked at his watch and nodded to Sam.

"Time for us to get going, Sam. You have classes this afternoon." Disappointment flashed across the teen's face. "Don't worry, you'll be back here soon enough. Charlie needs all the help he can get."

"Why do I feel like I've just been insulted?" Cooper asked as he slid an arm around Charlie's waist. "That was an insult, wasn't it?"

"No, love. Stu would *never* insult you. You're Cooper Evans. Award winning rock star. He wouldn't dare," Charlie deadpanned back.

Sam gave a giggle. "It was great to meet you, Cooper. And thanks, Charlie. I'm excited to come out and join you."

"You're welcome, Sam. You've got my card, so get your parents to call or email me, and we can work out the details," Charlie said as he shook Sam's hand. "Stu, are you coming to the barbeque on the weekend?"

"Of course I am. I wouldn't miss your mum and dad's annual get together for anything," Stu replied as he shook Charlie's hand. "I think B's on days though, so he'll be here later in the evening."

"Don't forget your gear. You can use one of the cottages so you don't have to drive home," Charlie told him as they walked out to the car.

"Looking forward to it. See you on the weekend." Stu waved goodbye as he drove away. Sam's excited chatter filled the car, and Stu let it wash over him, chasing away his earlier thoughts.

Chapter Thirteen

"You got a minute, Brett?"

Brett looked up from the incident report he was completing and nodded to his boss. "Sure. Give me a sec and I'll be right there." He quickly saved and closed the document and made his way into the adjoining office.

"What's up?"

Les waved a hand to the seat in front of his desk, and Brett sat down. The older man regarded him before he leaned forward, elbows resting on the surface.

"You've been in the service how long now? Twelve years?"

"Yeah, about that." Brett nodded in agreement.

"What are your thoughts, career wise? You're senior station officer qualified, but you've never applied for any available posts when they come up."

"I've always been happy here, with the team. And I know how hard it is to get an open position at another station. Like me, there are plenty of SSOs on the teams, and it's better to promote in-house than bring someone from another unit in."

"Would you ever consider moving out of Auckland?"

He'd never thought about moving away for his job, but now that Les had mentioned it, he was curious. "Why? Is there something coming up I should know about?"

"There could be," Les told him as he leaned back in his chair. "One of the guys in Hamilton is looking to retire early. His wife has had a bit of a health scare and he's thinking about moving his retirement up by six months."

"Is there no one down there qualified?"

"There is, but I thought of you when I heard about it earlier today. It would be a great opportunity for you.

You're more than capable and have the experience, and you've not really got anything keeping you here in Auckland, have you?"

"I…um…wow. I'm not sure what to say," he told Les honestly. It was true that he didn't have anything keeping him in Auckland. His parents and sister had moved three hours away to Mt Maunganui, and other than his job and friends, he had no other ties to the city. His stomach rolled at the thought of leaving his friends behind; well, one friend in particular.

"Hey, nothing is formalised yet. You've got time to think about applying when it becomes available, but I wanted you to start thinking about it. You're an excellent fire officer, Brett. I'd hate to see you go, but I also know you'd make an equally excellent station officer, and you need to get out of your comfort zone."

"Thanks, Les. That means a lot. I'll definitely give it some thought. Thanks for letting me know." Brett stood to leave. He needed a few minutes to get his head together.

Les nodded, dismissing him, and Brett made his way to the lunchroom to make himself a much needed coffee. He'd almost laughed out loud when Les had told him he needed to get out of his comfort zone. He'd certainly been doing that the last couple of weeks.

Memories of Stu's mouth on him had heat prickling under his skin. Things had been a little one-sided though. Stu had taken over, educating him and getting him off harder than he'd ever got off before in his life. He knew that Stu hadn't missed out though, but Brett had decided it was time to return the favour.

He was pulled from his thoughts by the sound of the alarm. He hastily swallowed the last of his coffee and raced towards the engine bay. As he jumped into the passenger seat, he switched off his thoughts and focused on the job at hand. He'd have plenty of time later to think things through.

Several hours later, he was pulling up beside the large farmhouse that Charlie's parents lived in. He'd thought he wouldn't get there in time for their annual Labour weekend barbeque. The call out to the car fire had dragged out when a spark had set fire to some nearby brush. Fortunately they had been able to get it under control quickly, and Brett was only a couple of hours behind schedule.

He could hear music and laughter from the back of the house and, pulling his fleece jacket on against the early spring chill, he made his way towards it, looking forward to a beer and the company of his friends.

His appearance raised a cheer and shouted greetings from the assembled group, and he took the time to hug and say hi to them all. Noticeable by his absence was Stu. Before he could ask where the missing man was though, he was being pulled to one side by Sarah.

"How are you, Brett?" the petite blonde asked as she gave him a tight hug.

"I'm good thanks, Sarah. How have you guys been?"

"Mia is crawling and into *everything,* and Mike and I are trying to keep up," she told him with a laugh.

"Where is the princess tonight?" Brett glanced around. There were several children running around and a few toddlers cuddling in their parent's arms.

"Mum and Dad have her. We've got a child-free night for once, and we're staying in Liz's cottage so we can both have a few drinks and not have to drive home or worry about waking with the sparrows in the morning."

They chatted for a few more minutes before they were interrupted by the rest of the gang.

"Hey, where's Stu?" Jase asked, craning his head to look around the crowd.

"Dunno. I haven't seen him since I got here." Brett shrugged. He'd been surreptitiously looking for the other man while chatting with Sarah.

"I saw him heading up to the house with that guy, Charlie, you know, your cousin's friend? About six-foot-tall and hot," Sarah said with a wink.

"Who? Tane?" Charlie asked.

Sarah gave a nod. "Yeah, that's the one. They were chatting up a storm." She gave an eyebrow waggle and a smirk. "Were looking very friendly."

Jealously shot through Brett and he took a deep swallow of his beer to hide his face. Rationally, he knew that Stu could talk to whomever he wanted to, but dammit, if his irrational side wasn't wanting him to march up to the house and tear Stu away.

He knew he and Stu had no official claim on each other. This was an experiment and a bit of fun. Certainly not a binding relationship—Stu didn't do those, unfortunately—and he himself wasn't sure he wanted to announce to their friends they were more than just buddies flatting together.

"You okay there, Brett?" Jase's voice broke into his thoughts.

"Yeah, why?"

"Oh, you just downed that beer rather quick. Looked like someone had pissed you off."

"Nah. All good. Just trying to catch up to you guys," he replied with a grin.

"Well, in that case, here, have another one," Cooper said with a laugh as he pushed a fresh bottle into his hands.

"You finally made it, B." Brett's heart lurched as Stu's voice came from behind him, and he quickly turned to see his best friend walking towards them, thankfully alone.

Brett ran his eyes over the familiar figure, ease settling over him when he confirmed that Stu didn't look like he'd been doing more than talking.

"Nice chat with Tane?" Sarah asked slyly.

"What? Oh yeah. He's just in his last year of his education degree and we were discussing what options he had," Stu replied, seemingly unaware of Sarah's innuendo.

"Oh. Is that all?" Sarah sounded disappointed.

"Yeah, why?" Stu frowned at her and then picked up on what Sarah was implying. "Oh, you thought we were sneaking off for a quickie round the back of the barn, weren't you?" Stu's eyes flicked briefly to Brett's, as if he was trying to gauge if Brett had thought the same thing. He returned his attention back to Sarah and gave her his usual cheeky grin. "Sorry to disappoint you, but no, we didn't do anything but talk. He's a very nice young man, but not for me."

Sarah gave a mock pout and grumbled about him being too fussy for his own good. As the teasing and laughs continued, Brett relaxed and enjoyed the company.

"So, guys. Do you have any plans for late February next year?" Cooper asked during a lull in the conversation.

There was a general chorus of *no's* and *whys?* from the group.

"Well, I'm kicking off my new tour here in Auckland in mid-February and then from early April I'm heading off to the United States for six weeks," he told them. Brett watched as the Englishman reached out to draw Charlie close to his side. "And the other night I proposed to Charlie, and we've decided to get married between the Australasian and US legs of the tour so he can come with me."

Sarah gave a squeal of delight as she rushed over to hug a grinning Charlie and Cooper. "I knew it!" she crowed before turning to her husband. "Pay up, Mike," she demanded, holding out her hand and waggling her fingers.

"What? You bet on them getting engaged? That was an easy bet. We *all* knew they were going to get married," Jase told her as he pulled Charlie into a congratulatory hug.

"No. I bet that you and Kyle would get engaged before Charlie and Coop," Mike said with a sigh.

Brett joined in the laughter before going to hug Charlie. "I'm so happy for you, mate," he told him. "You deserve this. Good on you."

"Thanks, Brett. I knew we'd end up married one day; he just beat me to the proposal." Charlie's features softened as he looked over to where Cooper was standing. "He's everything, and more than I ever wished for."

"Well, like I said, you deserve it," Brett repeated before going over to give Cooper a hug. "You look after him, you hear?" he mock warned.

Cooper returned the hug before looking Brett in the eye. "I promise with everything I am: he will always come first in my life."

Brett nodded and stepped away to let Stu congratulate the couple. Cooper's words gave him a sense of longing. He wanted what he and Charlie had. He wanted the easy laughs that Sarah and Mike had. He wanted what all his friends had—someone to love and who loved him back with all their being.

"Hey, you okay?" Stu asked quietly, nudging his shoulder.

"Yeah. Just tired," he lied.

Stu gave a quiet snort. "Try again, B. I know you better than that." He dropped his voice, turning slightly so the others couldn't see what he was saying. "In fact, I know you a lot better than this lot realise."

"I know you do," Brett replied. His gaze flicked to Stu's mouth before meeting his eyes. Stu gave him a knowing look in return.

"Do you want to disappear behind the barn for a quickie?" Stu teased quietly, letting his hand discreetly trace up the outer seam of Brett's jeans. Brett's breath hitched and he took a step away, willing his body not to react. The last thing he needed was his friends seeing him with a hard-on.

"Stop it," he growled quietly.

Stu chuckled and put his wayward hand back into his jacket pocket. "Okay, but, y'know, if you change your mind, just say the word."

Brett watched as he sauntered off towards the house and gave a sigh. He wanted Stu more than ever now. He'd thought that a few kisses and a couple of blowjobs would cure his infatuation and things would return to relative normality, but they hadn't. He wanted to ask someone what he should do now, but the one person he would normally talk to about it all, was the one person he couldn't.

Chapter Fourteen

Stu hummed quietly to himself as he made his way to the darkened cottage he was spending the night in. It had been a fun evening catching up with his friends, and the announcement of Cooper and Charlie's engagement had added to the festivities.

He was thrilled for his friends, glad they'd found their soulmates. He'd lost sight of Brett about an hour ago and figured his friend had just crashed early. He presumed the other man was staying in the cottage with him and had not driven home.

The familiar path was lit by watery moonlight and a cool breeze was blowing in off the sea below the rise. Stu pulled his jacket closer around him. Spring was taking its time to warm up this year, and he'd be glad to get into the house. He trod carefully along the side of the small building, his gaze focussing on where his feet were going when he was grabbed and tugged into the shadows.

He gave an unmanly yelp that was quickly smothered by the heat of Brett's mouth as it pressed against his. Overcoming his shock, Stu returned the kiss, his tongue duelling with Brett's as they fought for dominance. His brain demanded oxygen and he pulled away and took a heaving breath.

"What the fuck?" he managed to get out as Brett pushed up against him, forcing his back to hit the side of the house. Warm lips worked their way along his jaw and down his neck and a small moan escaped him.

Brett's body pressed against his, hands roaming his chest before settling on his waist and then around to his arse. Brett captured his mouth, pulling him in tight, and wandering hands squeezed and kneaded the muscles as Brett rubbed his groin against Stu's.

Stu's body responded the only way it could. He pushed his own erection against Brett's, internally cursing the denim barrier between them. He slid his fingers along the waistband of Brett's jeans, then up under the layers of hoodie and t-shirt to trace the smooth back. He felt goosebumps skitter across the exposed skin and a quiet whimper escaped Brett.

Part of Stu's brain was screaming at him to stop this, that they needed to get inside where he could strip Brett completely and take his time. The other part of his brain was getting off on the fact that Brett had cornered him and was taking control. So far, their make-out sessions and time in bed had largely been Stu in charge and leading the way. His lust-soaked brain decided he liked this side of Brett, and he couldn't wait to see where it would lead.

"B…we ne-need to…ah fuck, yes…" He started to say they needed to get inside, but Brett cupped his groin and squeezed him. It took all of Stu's willpower not to come there and then. "B…stop," he ground out as his traitorous body pushed against the hand rubbing him with firm strokes.

Brett stilled immediately, body tense. A shuddering breath escaped him, and he pulled from Stu, his gaze meeting Stu's briefly before dropping away.

"No, stay. You haven't done anything wrong," Stu rushed to reassure him, easily recognising the look of rejection that was quickly masked. He tugged at the front of Brett's fleece, and Brett took a reluctant step forward. Stu pressed a quick kiss to his swollen lips. "As usual, you were going to make me come. I just need a breather for a few seconds."

"Yeah?" Brett looked at him through his lashes, a small smile playing at the corner of his mouth.

"Don't look so fucking smug," Stu told him with an eye roll. "You know exactly what you were doing to me."

Brett chuckled and pressed himself against Stu and rolled his hips, causing Stu to bite back a moan.

"Exactly. Now, I think it would be a good idea if we took this inside as it's too bloody cold out here, and also, anyone could come along and catch us."

A puff of breath huffed against his neck as Brett sighed. "I know, but we're sharing the cottage with Kyle and Jase, and they're already in there. I've needed to kiss you all fucking night and knew this would be my only chance."

"Oh. I see," Stu said with a sigh. They certainly wouldn't be picking things back up once they got inside. Neither of them wanted their friends to know what was going on between them. He took Brett's face in his hands before kissing him again. This time wasn't as heated but sensual, and it lit up Stu's insides. He gently broke off with a few small pecks, and Brett gave him a rueful grin.

"Maybe not my best idea," Brett commented as he stepped away, adjusting his jeans.

"Hmm, maybe not. But there's no reason we can't pick up again tomorrow when we get home," Stu told him as they picked their way along the rough ground towards the path.

"True, but I'm back at work at five, and I…" Brett broke off.

"And you what?" Stu asked.

"There you are." Jase's voice came out of the darkness, halting any further discussion they may have had.

"Hey, you two. Where've you been?" Stu called out. "I thought you'd be all tucked up in bed by now?" He tugged his jacket tight around him, hoping he didn't look too dishevelled.

"Ah, yeah. Nah. We decided to have a quick walk along the…um…beach." As Jase and Kyle got closer, Stu could see that their clothes were not quite as straight as they should be, and Kyle's hair was all mussed up, as though fingers had been run through it many times. Kyle's full lips were also slightly puffy, and Stu bit back a grin.

"Don't blame you. It's a nice night, but it must be pretty cold down there," he told them as they all made their way into the cottage. The large lounge room was lit with a lamp, and Stu could see a faint redness staining Kyle's cheek he was sure wasn't from the wind.

"It was. We're just going to…ah…have a quick shower. To warm up," Jase told him as he pulled his boyfriend towards their room.

"Good idea. Don't want you getting sick or anything," Stu called after them. At the sound of the bathroom door closing, he burst into laughter.

"Those two couldn't be subtle if they tried," he told Brett. At Brett's slightly confused look, he quickly glanced down the hallway to ensure that Jase or Kyle weren't going to appear before pulling him in and kissing him soundly. "They've been doing on the beach what we were planning to do up here."

Understanding lit Brett's eyes and he gave a chuckle. "Well at least some of us are getting some tonight."

"Yeah, lucky bastards. Never mind, our turn will come," Stu told him as he made his way down the hallway. "See you in the morning, B."

At Brett's quiet *good night,* Stu closed his bedroom door.

*****

At breakfast the next morning, Brett found he had little appetite as he had to watch the guy from last night, Tane, monopolise Stu. Hemi, Charlie's dad had the barbeque going with bacon and eggs, and most of the guests that had stayed the night before were sitting down to eat.

Tane had seemed to be waiting for Stu to appear and had pulled him into an in-depth conversation, about what, Brett wasn't sure. What he was sure about was the fact he didn't like the way the younger man would touch Stu's arm and how he moved his chair slightly closer than was socially acceptable for someone you'd just met the night before at a family gathering.

Brett took a drink of his orange juice before turning his attention to his plate.

"So, Brett. Any ladies on the horizon we should know about?" Sarah asked from next to him.

"Nope. Not looking at the moment," he replied. Knowing Sarah, he wasn't going to be let off the hook.

"Really? Why not?" she asked, her gaze curious.

Brett shrugged. "Dunno. I'm busy with work and, y'know, just happy with my own company."

"That's not a bad thing, I suppose," Sarah conceded. "Taking time out for yourself, you know, to figure out what you want in life and where you're going, is a good thing. Means you'll be more open when the right person comes along."

"Yeah, you're right," Brett agreed, hoping it would appease Sarah's nosiness. He loved her dearly, but as the only female in their immediate circle of friends, she tended to mother them all. She meant well, but some days it was a bit much.

"Stu looks like he's got a fan there," she said, nodding towards the end of the table where the other man was sitting. He was listening intently to whatever Tane was saying to him, his blond hair contrasting sharply against the black hair of the younger man.

Brett gave a noncommittal grunt. He finished the last mouthful of food and pushed his plate away. He glanced at his watch and saw that he needed to make a move so he could get home and get organised before going on night shift later that afternoon.

"I'd better get going," he told Sarah. He leaned over and gave her a kiss on the cheek. "Thanks for the company."

"Anytime," she said, smiling at him. "You know you can talk to me any time, about anything, don't you, Brett?"

Brett smiled back at her and gave a small nod. "I'm all good, thanks, Sarah."

She didn't look convinced but let him go with a pat to his hand. He quickly made the rounds of the table, thanking Hemi and Jo Samuels for their hospitality and then said goodbye to his friends with promises to catch up with them later in the week once his night shifts had finished.

He finally ended up where Stu was sitting and noticed with some irritation that Tane's knee was brushing against Stu's. Stu seemed oblivious, intent on listening to whatever the other man was saying. Brett cleared his throat, and Stu looked up, a grin forming on his face.

"Sorry to interrupt," Brett said, nodding to the two of them, "but I'm heading home. Just thought I'd check if there's anything you want from the supermarket as I've got to get some stuff."

"Is it that time already?" Stu asked, pulling his phone from his pocket to check. He smiled up at Brett. "I can't think of anything, but if I do, I'll text you."

"Okay. I'll see you at home then. Unless, of course, you're not coming straight home, and I'll see you in a couple of days."

"I won't be too far behind you," Stu told him. "I've got some stuff to prep before work tomorrow, so I'll be leaving shortly."

Brett couldn't help the small thrill of satisfaction that went through him at the look of disappointment that crossed Tane's face. With a nod to them both, he strode towards his truck, feeling a little lighter than he had earlier that morning.

Chapter Fifteen

The loud pop of crushed metal giving way to the Jaws of Life had Brett sighing in relief as the final pieces of the door frame released from the main body of the car. The machine was cumbersome, and he took a cautious step back to allow the other members of his team to position themselves to lift the roof from the wrecked vehicle. As soon as it was off, an ambulance officer was leaning into the car to check on the moaning driver.

Brett made his way to the fire truck and returned the life-saving equipment to its spot. He did a sweep of the area, noting the police marking out the positions of the other vehicles involved. It was two in the morning, and Brett and his team had been on the go with three other call outs since they had signed on eight hours earlier. He suppressed a yawn and tried not to think too longingly of his bed. As the ambulance pulled away, he was grateful that he was heading home later and not to the hospital.

"Brett, I'm going to send the other units back to base. You and your team are on clean up once the cops have finished and the towie's have been given the okay to take the wrecks away," Les told him.

"Any news on the people in the minivan?" he asked his boss as the other crews began clearing and checking their equipment.

"Driver is priority two critical. Female passenger from the front seat not much better. Thankfully the kids in the back just have cuts and bruises. Other family members were travelling behind them, so they are taking care of them." Les shook his head ruefully. "It's the same at the end of every long weekend. People travel late to avoid the traffic and then fall asleep at the wheel."

"Do we know that's what happened?" Brett asked.

"Cops are ninety percent sure after talking to some of the witnesses, but no doubt they will confirm it after the Serious Crash Unit has done their investigation."

Brett waved his boss and the other crews off and then set about helping where he could to get the remnants of the accident cleared away. Nearly two hours later, the final mangled vehicle was taken away by the tow trucks, and Brett and his team swept up the mess of broken glass and twisted metal scattered across the road. Once the worst had been picked up, they hosed the tarmac down to clear away any surface oil and fuel. Brett had a short conversation with the remaining police officer, who declared the road clear to be opened, and the crew were able to make their way back to the station.

Brett was bone tired by the time he got home. He was almost too tired to eat but knew that if he didn't, he'd wake up in a couple of hours hungry and then his whole body clock would be thrown out of whack for the rest of the day.

He stumbled into the kitchen and stopped short when he saw a plate with crispy bacon and an egg sitting on the bench. He blinked as Stu pressed a mug of hot tea into his hand and didn't resist when he was made to sit on the bar stool at the counter.

"What's all this for?" he asked, confused.

"Heard on the radio about the accident last night and figured you'd have been there. I knew you'd be tired when you got home, so thought I'd do you some breakfast before you crash," Stu told him as he quickly tidied up after himself.

"Thanks, Stu. I owe you one."

Stu gave a wave of his hand as he reached for his travel mug. "You can repay the favour later," he said with a wink.

Brett caught his arm as Stu brushed past him. "Oh, I will, don't you worry," he informed him before brushing his lips across Stu's.

Stu leaned in and deepened the kiss for a moment before pulling away. "I was thinking more of you cooking dinner, but I'll take anything else you're offering too."

"Go to work. You'll be late." Brett shooed him off, his earlier weariness slipping away at his friend's thoughtfulness. "Have a good day, dear," he called out and was rewarded with a reply of *fuck off* as the front door closed.

Brett made short work of the bacon and eggs and then headed to the shower. Feeling clean and a lot more relaxed, he slid into bed where he fell into a deep sleep within minutes.

*****

"Mr Johnson, sir. Do you have a second?"

Stu turned at the sound of Sam's voice as he walked across the courtyard towards the classroom block. The teenager was grinning, and happiness radiated off him. His friend Jack was with him, quietly watching on.

"Of course, I do, Sam. What can I do for you?"

"I just wanted to let you know that I start work with Charlie next week. My mum and dad went out to meet him, and they've said it's okay for me to work for him and everything."

"That's good news, Sam. I'm really happy for you. Charlie is a great guy, and you'll learn a lot from him," Stu said, pleased that his friend had been able to help.

"Yeah, Mrs Samuels has said I can stay in one of the rooms at her house so I don't have to drive back and forth every day. Charlie showed them the house he's working on, and they were super impressed," Sam told him excitedly. "They couldn't believe I'd be helping on Coo—I mean, such a huge project."

"Jo and Hemi Samuels will look after you. I was out there myself this weekend. They have a big family barbecue every Labour weekend and are great hosts."

"Mum was relieved when she met them. I think that's what swayed them into saying yes. And meeting Cooper."

"Who's Cooper?" Jack interrupted and a dull flush spread across Sam's face as he realised what he'd said.

"He's…ah…Charlie's boyfriend," Sam stammered as he sent an imploring look at Stu.

"It's okay, Sam. I'm sure Charlie and Coop won't mind you telling your best friend, but please don't tell anyone else," Stu told them sternly.

"What's so special about this Cooper guy?" Jack asked, looking between the two of them.

Sam gave a sigh and pulled his phone out of his pocket. He tapped the screen, and Stu caught a glimpse of a selfie of the teenager with a grinning Cooper. "Before I show you this, you have to promise not to say a word to anyone. Please, Jack. This is important to me."

"I promise," Jack reassured him. Sam slowly handed him the phone, and Stu bit back a laugh when realisation dawned on Jack who his best friend was talking about. "Is this…is that…Cooper Evans? You're working on Cooper Evans's house?"

"Yeah, and you can't say anything, okay?"

Jack gaped at the phone and then looked at Stu suspiciously. "So does that mean you're friends with Cooper, Mr Johnson?"

"Yes, I suppose I am. His boyfriend Charlie and I have been friends since our university days, and I met Cooper last summer when he came out here to stay," Stu said, trying to hide his smile.

Before Jack could ask any more questions, the bell for the next class period rang. "Okay, you two, off to class. Good luck for next week, Sam, and I'll see you back here for your English exam."

The boys grinned before heading off down the corridor to their next class, and Stu made his way to his own. He thumbed a quick message to Charlie to thank him for taking Sam on. Before he could put his phone away, a text came through from Brett.

Brett: *Hey. Fish okay for dinner?*

Stu: *Yes, if you're cooking. Need me to pick anything up?*

Brett: *No thanks. I'm at the supermarket now. See you later.*

Stu sent back a quick 'thumbs up' emoji and then got his class of thirteen-year-olds settled down.

Arriving home a few hours later, he found an episode of Game of Thrones playing on the TV and a lightly snoring Brett stretched out on the couch with Cap and Bucky curled up on his feet and chest, respectively. Stu bit back a grin and gave into the temptation of snapping a photo. After changing out of his work clothes, he grabbed beers from the fridge and wandered back into the lounge. Brett hadn't moved, and Stu knew that if he didn't wake up soon, he'd never sleep later and would be even more tired and grumpy the following day.

He put the beers on the coffee table and crouched down next to the couch. Brett's features were relaxed in sleep, his lips slightly parted, and Stu had a sudden need to feel them against his own. He gently brushed a wayward strand of hair from Brett's brow before leaning forward and lightly kissing him. It was only a soft brush, and Brett gave a slight twitch and a sigh.

With a smile, Stu did it again, pressing a little firmer and for longer. This time as he pulled away, Brett's chin lifted, as if chasing Stu's mouth, before the tip of his tongue licked across his bottom lip. Stu stifled a groan at the sight and, balancing himself with an arm on the back of the couch, leaned down and kissed Brett again, causing the cats to jump away and disappear out of the room.

The response he got was a soft moan as Brett's mouth parted under his. Stu didn't notice the hand grasping the front of his shirt, just the realisation he was being pulled off balance and onto Brett's chest. Strong arms wrapped around him and legs shifted until Stu was lying on top of Brett, their mouths never losing touch for a second.

Brett broke the kiss, his hands on either side of Stu's face. "Hi," he said, his voice husky from sleep and arousal.

"Hi, yourself," Stu replied, grinning down at him. "Have a good nap?"

"Mmm hmm," Brett hummed as he pulled Stu back down. "Thank you for waking me," he murmured against Stu's mouth before kissing him again.

Stu let Brett take control of the kiss. It wasn't too slow or too rushed. They took their time exploring each other's mouths, and Stu gave a small groan as Brett's calloused hand ran under his t-shirt and up his spine. Suddenly he wanted more skin on skin. He broke the kiss and leaned back on his haunches to pull his shirt off.

Brett looked up at him, eyes dark with arousal and mouth soft and slightly swollen. After throwing his shirt onto the floor, he tugged at Brett's, and with a slight grin, Brett hunched forward so Stu could tug it over his head.

Stu settled back onto Brett, revelling in the feel of the rasp of chest hair against his own smooth skin. He kissed along Brett's collarbone and nibbled up his neck, sucking gently at the tender spot below his ear. Brett hadn't shaved, he rarely did when he was on his days off, and the soft scrape of stubble sent a tingle down Stu's spine.

Brett arched up into him whilst pulling at Stu's hips to get their erections closer. God, Stu loved this. He loved the way Brett responded to him. He rutted against the firm body below him as he captured Brett's mouth again.

"Want you," he murmured against Brett's mouth.

Brett groaned in response. "Hmmm. Bedroom. Now."

They untangled themselves and got to their feet. The trip to the bedroom involved Brett plastered to Stu's back, arms wrapped around his chest, mouth at his neck, and stiff cock rubbing against his arse.

They stumbled into the bedroom, Stu turning to capture Brett's mouth again as he was edged towards the bed. When his legs bumped into the edge, he tore his mouth away from Brett's and pushed him backwards.

"Strip," he commanded as he got rid of his sweatpants. Brett made quick work of his zipper and soon his jeans were lying in a heap. They fell onto the bed, rutting and touching. Stu gasped as Brett's hand wrapped around his cock and stroked from base to tip. He started to ease Brett onto his back, but Brett pushed back and rolled on top of Stu.

"My turn," he rasped out huskily.

"What do you mean?" Stu started to ask but then froze as Brett gave him a wicked grin and began kissing his way down Stu's chest. As the hot mouth got to his stomach, he realised what Brett meant. "Wait. B, are you sure? You don't have to, you know."

Lust-filled eyes met his. "I'm very sure. I've been thinking of doing this for days. Now shut up and enjoy." With that, he shuffled further down the bed and nudged Stu's thighs apart so he could settle between them.

Stu gave a muted groan at the sight of his best friend between his legs and dropped his head back onto the pillow.

Chapter Sixteen

Brett stared at the erect cock in front of him. It was slightly shorter and wider than his and cut, unlike his own. A thick vein ran down its length to where it disappeared into a neatly trimmed thatch of dark blond curls.

"It's just a dick, B. You have one of your own, y'know," Stu said in amusement. Brett shifted his gaze to meet the laughing blue eyes of the man spread out before him.

"I've never looked at one from this angle before," Brett replied, tilting his head and peering at the dick in question.

"Are you squinting? Why are you squinting?" Stu's voice rose an octave as he pushed himself up onto his elbows.

Brett laughed and ran his thumb up the length before circling the crown and gently rubbing the sensitive spot just below it.

Stu hissed and dropped back to the bed. "Remember, you don't have to do this. You don't have to do anything you don't want to."

"I told you, I've been thinking about this for days. Now lie back and enjoy."

Stu huffed out a laugh, which changed to a moan as Brett tilted his cock towards his mouth and ran his tongue tentatively up the pulsing vein.

He tasted bitter salt and it wasn't unpleasant. Feeling a little surer of himself, he did it again, this time lingering at the crown. A sudden burst of salty liquid across his tongue had his mouth watering, and without thought, he began sucking.

Stu whimpered and his hips jerked up in reflex, pushing himself further into Brett's mouth. Brett tensed for a second before easing his mouth off and pressing kisses down the straining shaft. He nuzzled into the crease of Stu's thigh, inhaling the scent of musk and the faint remnants of the body wash Stu had used that morning. His own cock jerked, and he ground his hips into the bed, seeking friction.

He flicked a glance up to find Stu watching him with heat in his eyes. Brett winked at him before sucking him back into his mouth. He went a little further this time, letting the thick cock fill his mouth. He knew he wouldn't be able to deep throat like Stu, so he stroked what he couldn't fit into his mouth with one hand while his other hand fondled and teased Stu's balls.

The jerk of Stu's hips plus the whimpers coming from the top of the bed were increasing Brett's own desire. He'd always found the most pleasure in pleasing his lover and this time was no different. A short tug on his hair stopped him, and he slowly let Stu's cock slide out of his mouth.

"I'm close, B," Stu panted out, his fair skin flushed.

Brett swirled his tongue around the top of Stu's dick for one final taste before crawling up the bed and taking the other man's mouth in a sloppy, open-mouthed kiss. Stu's fingers dug into Brett's hips, pulling him as close as he could. They began to rut against each other, the need for friction and release making them oblivious to everything except each other.

Brett balls tightened and he was torn between pushing a little further to achieve orgasm and holding back, wanting—needing—Stu to get off first. He ran a palm down Stu's ribcage and slipped a hand between their straining bodies. He'd just wrapped his hand around Stu's heated cock when Stu tensed beneath him and threw his head back as he came. Stu gripped Brett's shoulder, short nails pressing into his skin. With his eyes closed and lower lip caught between his teeth as tremors wracked through his body, Brett didn't think he'd seen a sexier sight, and that, along with the heat of Stu's come slicking against their bellies, had Brett spilling his own release.

Both men continued to rub against each other, but a lot slower, until they were oversensitive, and Brett rolled onto his back, throwing an arm across his eyes. He'd had another earth-shattering orgasm. It didn't matter how many times they did this; he always came hard and intensely. That had probably happened about a couple of dozen times in his whole adult life prior to this. Surely it wouldn't last? Surely it was the novelty of a new lover, and a male lover at that?

"Geez, what does a guy need to do to get dinner around here?" Stu's teasing voice broke into his thoughts.

Lifting his arm, he turned his head and gave his friend a flat look. "You started it."

"And you definitely finished it," Stu said as he reached for the packet of wipes on the bedside table. He tore a couple out of and wiped himself down before repeating the action on Brett.

"You complaining?" Brett asked, fighting a yawn as a wave of fatigue and post orgasm lethargy hit him.

"Not about the sex, no. About the lack of dinner? Definitely."

"Jeez. Give a guy a blowjob and he still complains," Brett grumbled without heat. He knew Stu was winding him up.

Stu leaned over him, eyes searching his face. "About that. You okay?"

"Of course, I am. Why wouldn't I be?"

"Um…because you just gave your first blowjob?"

"You complaining?" Brett asked again, this time with a quirk of his eyebrow.

"Hell, no. Wasn't a bad effort for your first attempt," Stu told him with a grin before jumping away as Brett lunged for him.

"If you think I'm cooking dinner now, you're shit out of luck," Brett told him as he pushed himself off the bed.

"We'll compromise and cook together. Then we might look at improving your technique," Stu taunted sassily as he disappeared out of the room.

Brett chuckled to himself as he pulled on his jeans. He could hear Stu talking to Bucky and Cap as he fed them. He could get behind that idea.

*****

Stu pretended not to notice the small pieces of fish Brett was sneaking to the cats winding around their ankles as they worked in companionable silence to prepare dinner. He rinsed off the lettuce leaves and began tearing them before starting on the other ingredients for the salad. He jumped slightly when the warm pressure of Brett's hands squeezed his hips to move him to the side to reach into the drawer Stu was standing in front of. Brett chuckled and pressed a brief kiss to the back of his neck before returning to the other side of the kitchen, which send a flood of warmth through him. He and Brett had cooked together many times over the years. In fact, it had been Brett's mother who'd taught him to cook, the skill not something his own mother had, or the inclination to share if she did. But in all their years of working together, there had never been this level of intimacy, and Stu wasn't sure how he felt about it.

His whole relationship with Brett had changed now they were sleeping together. The core of their friendship was still there, but now he was more aware when Brett entered the room, and when they were out, he found himself looking for the familiar sight of his best friend. Even on the weekend, at the Samuels' barbecue, he'd realised he could have had a quickie behind the barn with Tane, as Sarah had alluded to, but had chosen to ignore the subtle cues the younger man had been sending him.

"You finished over there?" Brett's question broke into Stu's thoughts. Stu looked down to see he had been holding the knife but not using it. He finished slicing the tomatoes and added them to the bowl with the other ingredients.

"Yep. Is the fish ready?"

"Already plated, mate. Where were you? You looked like you were miles away." Brett said, passing him a plate with a piece of golden pan-fried fish.

"Yeah, sorry. Just running over some work stuff," he lied, giving Brett a quick smile as he added salad to his plate. He grabbed cutlery and his beer and headed for the dining table.

After dinner they took their usual places at each end of the couch. Brett flicked on the television and surfed through the channels like a seasoned professional. Stu opened his phone and scrolled through the various social media sites but with little interest. His mind kept going back to Brett and what they were doing. *What were they doing?* Things had gone past an experimental kiss and hand job. Now he was initiating sex and so was Brett. The blowjob earlier had been a little sloppy and unpractised, but it had also been one of the best he'd had. *But why?* He'd had some earth-shattering blowjobs in the past, from some very experienced guys, but the one he'd got earlier in the evening had made him feel like he was the only guy in the world to have ever been given head.

It didn't make sense. Was it because there was an emotional connection between him and Brett? His previous partners had always been one- or two-night stands. The only time he'd had a relationship in any sense of the word was his first year at university with another guy who'd recently come out and was figuring out things. They'd practiced and experimented with each other, and in their second semester, both had moved on to other guys.

His social media meandering paused as he saw a post from Cooper on his official Instagram account announcing his engagement to Charlie. There was a great candid shot of them laughing at something off screen and the photo credit was given to Lizzie, Charlie's sister. He liked the post and closed his phone down.

He didn't do relationships. He'd never felt a yearning to have someone in his life permanently. He had his friends and his career. He was happy. *Wasn't he?* He'd always had to fend for himself. His parents had been—and still were—so busy with their own careers, he'd learnt to amuse himself from an early age. There had been a procession of nannies and au-pairs when he was younger, and as he got into his teens, his parents more or less left him to his own devices, which was why he'd spent so much time at Brett's place.

A nudge of feet against his thigh dragged him out of his thoughts to find Brett watching him with a frown on his face.

"You're quiet tonight. Are you sure everything is okay?"

"Yeah. Just tired. You know what it's like as we get towards the end of the year," Stu said.

"Are you upset…y'know, about before?" Brett asked, nodding towards the bedroom.

"What? No. Of course not," Stu rushed to reassure him. "It was fine, I mean great," Stu quickly corrected himself as he saw Brett wince at his word choice. "Sorry, I'm just really tired. I'm going to turn in early. Thanks for dinner." As he stood, the cats took it as a signal and jumped up from where they were lying to race down the hallway.

"Oh. Okay then." Disappointment flashed across Brett's face before it was hidden and he slouched down into the couch, shoulders hunching.

Stu hesitated. He knew he'd told Brett they could go another round, but he needed some time to sort through his thoughts.

"G'night, B," he said softly before leaving the room.

Chapter Seventeen

"Thanks for dropping in the builder's report from Charlie," Jase said as he handed Brett a beer before slumping onto the couch.

"No problem," Brett replied. "Made sense for me to bring it back rather than Charlie drive all the way in, especially with him being so busy."

"Cooper's house is looking good though, isn't it?" Jase took a mouthful of beer.

"Charlie's done an amazing job." Brett nodded to the sheaf of paperwork on the table. "So, you and Kyle have found a place then?"

Jase grinned. "Yeah. An old villa up on the hill overlooking St Heliers, so close to here. It's recently been renovated, and we wanted Charlie to do a quick check over for us that everything is up to scratch."

"So, you've made an offer?"

"Yep. We saw it last weekend and put an offer in on Monday and it was accepted pretty much straight away. We've made it subject to a builder's report, and if Charlie is happy with it, then it will go unconditional next Friday."

"When will you move?"

"All going well, in a month's time."

"That's great news. I'm really happy for you," Brett told him as he raised his beer in a toast. "It's all happening, isn't it? Charlie and Coop getting engaged, you and Kyle buying a place."

Jase looked at him quizzically. "Are you okay? You seem a little down?"

Brett plastered a smile on his face, but knew he'd failed in convincing his friend when Jase lifted an eyebrow at him. He heaved out a sigh and leaned back in his chair.

"I'm just feeling left behind, I suppose," he admitted. "I mean, I'm thirty-one, have been in the same job since I finished school, don't have a house of my own, and I dunno; I guess I'm feeling I should be further on in my life."

"Okay. I can understand why you'd feel like that. I thought you loved your career?"

"I do. I really can't imagine doing anything else, but you know you get some days when you wonder why you do it at all?" Brett looked at Jase, who nodded but didn't reply. "And as for having a home of my own, with the ridiculous house prices in Auckland, I certainly don't have a chance of getting anything halfway decent with the small deposit I've got."

"I agree with you on the house prices," Jase said. "Unfortunately, it's how it is these days."

"Says the multi-millionaire," Brett teased with a smile.

Jase had the grace to blush. "Hmm, true. We haven't had to worry about a mortgage. But I help a lot of people through the Sherwood Trust with property investment, and I know it sounds silly, but maybe looking at a place out of Auckland and renting it out may be an option."

"My boss mentioned there's a position coming up at a station in Hamilton early next year. I could kill two birds with one stone."

"You'd consider leaving Auckland?" Jase asked, surprised.

"Maybe? I don't have a lot holding me here. I mean, there's you guys and the blokes on my team, but with Mum and Dad now living down at Mt Maunganui with my sister, there's really nothing to anchor me here."

The sound of the front door opening had Jase's attention switch from their conversation, and Brett watched with some amusement as Jase's face lit up with happiness.

"Hey, darlin'" Kyle said as he walked into the room. Brett took a moment to admire how good the Texan looked in his dark grey suit. With his classic American boy-next-door looks, he was an attractive man, and with Brett's new awareness, he could appreciate why Jase was head over heels. Kyle leaned down over the back of the couch to kiss his boyfriend, and Brett dropped his eyes from the couple as memories of kissing Stu filled his mind. He'd missed not seeing or touching Stu for the last three days that he'd been at Charlie and Cooper's, but after Stu's dismissal the other night, insecurity had set in and he'd felt it better to let Stu have some space to work through whatever was on his mind.

"Hi, Kyle. Bye, Kyle," he said as they broke apart.

"Hey Brett," Kyle replied, shaking Brett's hand. "No need to rush off just because I'm home. Stay and join us for dinner if you've got no plans."

"Nah, you're all good. I know you've been away for a couple of days and I'm sure you'd be happier without me here."

"Don't be stupid, stick around," Jase said. "We haven't had a proper catch up in ages. We can order in from that new Thai place up the road. You'll love the duck dish they do."

Brett considered the offer. It wasn't like he was going to get a huge welcome when he got home, and Jase and Kyle were easy company.

"Okay, then. If you're sure?" he asked, looking between both men. At their nods, he agreed. "I'll stay for dinner, but I will have to head home straight after as I'm on shift in the morning."

"Great. Darlin', you order while I get changed," Kyle said as he loosened his tie and disappeared down the hallway to their bedroom.

As they ate, the three men caught up on their news. Jase and Kyle shared more details of their house and the plans for Kyle's family upcoming visit over Christmas. After a couple of hours of chat and banter, Brett said his goodbyes and made his way home.

He quietly let himself in, noting that Stu was either not in or had gone to bed. He felt some tension leave his body. He didn't know why he was so nervous about seeing Stu. Part of it was probably because he'd done what he'd promised he wouldn't do and had disappeared off to Charlie's again and had only messaged Stu to let him know he'd be back that night. Of course, his unplanned visit with Jase and Kyle meant he was later than he'd planned to be. He'd been hurt when Stu had been distracted during dinner and afterwards while watching TV. He knew his friend had been lying when he said he had work things on his mind. He wasn't sure what had scared Stu off, but he'd felt dismissed and rejected at Stu's early exit. Maybe it was time to end things now, before they went further? Brett winced at the thought.

*****

Stu glanced at the clock on the wall and sighed when he saw it was only five minutes later than the last time he'd looked. He mentally slapped himself. Brett would be home soon. He couldn't work out why he was so eager to see him. *Liar.* He knew exactly why he couldn't wait to see the other man. He'd missed him and add in the fact he was horny and wanted nothing more than to be all over Brett the minute he walked through the door. He only had himself to blame though, with his behaviour after the blowjob the other night.

Brett had messaged him three days ago to let him know he was working out at Charlie's and that he'd return on Friday night sometime. Knowing that his shift started the following morning, Stu had expected his flatmate home early evening, but now it was close to ten o'clock and there was no sign of him.

For the first time ever, Stu's home had not been the haven of peace it normally was but had felt empty and hollow without Brett there. There were signs of his presence, his old sneakers by the door, a hoodie that had gotten mixed up with Stu's laundry, but he'd missed his flatmate more than he'd expected to.

Deciding he was being pathetic by sitting and waiting, Stu headed for bed. He settled against the pillows and tried to read his book. For once, even the lure of a good story couldn't stop his concentration from wandering, and after he'd read the same line four times, he shut off his Kindle and lay back.

He tried some deep breathing exercises, but his mind still raced. He knew he fucked up the other night, but this thing with Brett was going further than he'd expected. But the thought of not continuing made him unsettled. His thoughts often drifted to Brett, the feel of him under him, over him. The taste of him and, god, the amount of times in the last few days he'd relived the blowjob Brett had given him. He wanted another one, more than one. He wanted Brett's mouth all over him and he wanted to return the favour. He wanted more than just experimenting.

The sound of the front door opening had Stu sitting up. He heard Brett creep up the hallway and the quiet snick of his bedroom door closing. He heaved a sigh and flopped back down onto the bed. *Tomorrow,* he vowed, *he would sit Brett down and tell him he wanted more. That he wanted to continue what they were doing.* Resolution made, he willed himself to sleep.

Chapter Eighteen

Stu and Brett eyed each other from across the couch, tension thick in the air. They knew they needed to talk, but both were reluctant to start. Stu put his empty mug on the coffee table and pulled Bucky into his lap as a distraction. The cat gave him a baleful glare, not happy to be removed from his spot.

"So, I've been thinking," Stu started.

"Yeah, me too." He ran a hand through hair, and Stu recognised the nervous gesture. Before Stu could say any more, Brett continued. "I think it's time to stop this thing, this experiment, that we've been doing."

All of Stu's prepared speech dissolved and white noise filled his head. He hadn't been expecting Brett to want to call things off. "I…ah….yeah, of course, you're right." He gave what he hoped was a reassuring nod and smile. "So, you've…um…you're okay with what we've done? Where we're at?"

"Yes. You've made me see that I'm probably bisexual. I mean, I haven't looked at any other guys, but now I know that I'm comfortable being with a guy, I can broaden my horizons, so to speak."

At Brett's words, pain shot through Stu's chest and he unconsciously pressed a hand to his breastbone. Stu didn't want Brett with another man. In fact, he didn't want him with anyone else, regardless of their gender. Brett was his. *Oh, shit!* He tried to keep breathing normally when it felt like he was drowning. *Why did it hurt to breathe?* This is why he didn't do relationships. He knew he'd end up hurt and alone. He wasn't boyfriend material. He wasn't worth Brett's love. *Love?* His mind skittered away from the thought. He couldn't be in love. *Could he?*

"Stu, are you okay?" Brett's concerned voice broke into his thoughts. He gave a start, and Bucky jumped off his lap at the sudden movement, pinching him with the tips of his claws in retribution.

"Yeah, uh, I'm fine," Stu managed to get out. He needed to escape. He needed to figure out what was happening. He wanted to curl up in a ball and hide from the world. He gave Brett a smile that probably looked as fake as it felt. "You're right. It's probably for the best."

"I mean, it's not like you want a relationship, is it, and honestly, could you see us doing the whole boyfriend thing?" Brett gave a chuckle, as though the thought amused him.

Stu forced a laugh. "True. Let's leave all that shit to the other guys, eh?" He stood up shakily. "I'm going to head out for a bit. I'll catch you later?"

"Stu? Are we, you know, okay?" A worried look crossed Brett's face.

"Of course, we are," he said, slapping a hand on Brett's shoulder, trying not to let it turn into a caress. "Be safe out there the next few days. I know it's always crazy when the fireworks go on sale."

Brett looked like he was going to say something else, so Stu gave him a quick smile before walking away. He grabbed his keys and wallet from the hall table and tried not to slam the front door on his way out. He probably shouldn't drive, but he needed to get as far away as he could. Reversing out of the driveway, he turned his car towards the beach and drove away.

*****

Brett watched his oldest friend walk away and felt bereft. Stu had seemed a little shaken, which surprised Brett. He'd thought he would have been relieved that Brett had called a halt to their experiment before things got complicated. He'd thought Stu would have been excited for him and eagerly planning a night out to test Brett's theory.

The thing was, though, Brett couldn't imagine being with anyone but Stu. Although he'd finally admitted to himself that he was bisexual and was open to being with either a girl or a guy, it was Stu that he imagined being with, and he really didn't know how that was going to work. He wasn't someone that did casual, and Stu was. He didn't want to give up his closest friend, so this was the only way. He knew he'd only end up being hurt if he and Stu carried on as they were. He'd lose his heart and then wouldn't be able to be around Stu. It would get awkward for their friends. He groaned and scrubbed his hands through his hair. He'd made the right decision, the only decision. So why did it feel so wrong?

The next few days passed in a flurry of busy shifts as Guy Fawkes night rolled around. The days leading up to the traditional celebration of the bombing of the UK parliament centuries ago were always manic. Fireworks could only be sold and purchased for the three days before November 5th and people spent more money than they should to see it go up in smoke. It was always one of the busiest nights of the year, and even falling midweek didn't deter the idiots who thought they knew how to handle an explosive device. Brett and his team were out on calls more than they were in the station. Brett was grateful he had the following Saturday off as it would be just as crazy come the weekend with belated parties being held.

After catching up on his sleep, he once again headed out to Charlie's to help with the renovation on Cooper's house. He spent three days doing as much as could, burying himself in work. Rather than spend his evenings with the loved-up couple, he used the time to scour the real estate sites for places to rent. As much as he hated the thought, he needed to move out from Stu's sooner rather than later. They needed distance to allow them to get back to normal.

He also took Jase's suggestion and looked at houses in Hamilton. Buying a property there was certainly more achievable than in Auckland. He decided he would talk to his boss, Les, when he went back on shift about the upcoming vacancy down there. It was time to grow up and be an adult. His friends would always be his friends. He wouldn't lose them if he moved. His head knew this was the best decision for him, but his gut twisted every time he thought of moving away.

His phone beeped with an incoming message, pulling him away from his introspection and the real estate website. It was from his mother, reminding him it was his father's birthday the following week and asking if he was still coming to visit as planned months ago.

With a sigh, Brett replied in the affirmative. He had forgotten that his dad's birthday was so soon. A few days with his family was just the distraction he needed.

Chapter Nineteen

The high-pitched squeal of nearly one-year-old Mia Lawson rang across the general murmur of conversation taking place over brunch at her parents' house. Stu couldn't help but grin as Jase blew another raspberry on her belly, causing her to giggle uncontrollably. The sound was infectious, and the adults around the table joined in at the delight the little girl was displaying.

Jase was truly smitten with his goddaughter, and Stu knew it wouldn't be long before Jase and Kyle began talking marriage and children. They may have told everyone their new, bigger house was for when Kyle's family visited from Texas, but they all knew it was so the couple could start their own. Stu shot a glance at Cooper and Charlie and noticed the affectionate looks they had. Yep, wouldn't be long before they began talking kids either.

For the first time ever, Stu felt a pang of jealousy. He'd never thought about having children as that usually involved having a permanent partner, and he'd never been in the market for one of those. Not that he was really in the market for one now. The only person he wanted to have as a partner didn't want him, and he wasn't going to try to fill the Brett-shaped hole in his heart with anyone else.

He'd attempted to carry on as normal since his and Brett's conversation the previous week. He'd gone through the motions at school and spent his evenings working his way through end-of-year reports. Brett had again been conspicuous by his absence. First by being at work and then going out to Cooper's place.

"Earth to Stu, come in Stu!" Sarah's voice broke into his thoughts, and he looked up to see the smirking faces of his friends.

"What? Sorry. I was miles away."

"Yeah, you were. What's up, mate? You've been distracted all morning," Jase asked him.

"Oh nothing." Stu waved a hand in dismissal. "Just my brain running over everything that has to be done this week. You know how I am at this time of year," he said, hoping they'd accept the lie.

Sarah gave him a look that suggested she wasn't buying his bullshit but thankfully didn't call him on it.

"How's the packing going?" he asked Jase and Kyle, hoping the change in topic would distract the group from questioning him further.

"Ugh. I didn't realise how much junk I'd accumulated in the five years I've been in the place," Jase told him before grinning at his boyfriend. "And I can't even blame it on being half of Kyle's crap as he's got his stuff from the States in a storage unit."

"It's a great opportunity to have a good sort out though," Sarah informed him as she cleared their plates from the table.

"I'd hate to move now," Stu agreed. "My books alone took more boxes than should be legally allowed when I moved in, and that was ten years ago. I've got even more now and packing them up would be a nightmare."

"Has Brett found anywhere new to live yet?" Charlie asked.

Stu shrugged to cover the lurch his stomach gave. "Not that he's mentioned to me," he admitted. "But, then again, if he's not at work at the station, he's out at Cooper's place, so I doubt he's had time." Stu took a deep drink from his coffee, trying to gather himself before continuing. "Not that there's any rush. I don't mind him being at my place."

"If he gets that job in Hamilton, he'll be able to afford to buy a house down there," Jase said as he stood to pass a now sleepy Mia to her father.

Stu choked on the mouthful of coffee he'd just swallowed. "Hamilton? What job in Hamilton?"

"Y'know, the station officer job that his boss told him about?" Jase said with a frown.

Stu shook his head slowly. "No, he hasn't said anything to me about a job in Hamilton."

"Oh, shit. Maybe I wasn't supposed to say anything," Jase said, horrified. "Oh god. Please don't let on you know. He may have not wanted to tell you until it was done and dusted."

"Yeah, that's probably it. Don't worry, mate. I won't say a word until he does."

"He has been unusually quiet this week," Charlie said, and Cooper nodded in agreement.

"Yeah, he didn't hang with us like he normally does after dinner. He always headed back to the cottage," Cooper added.

"Well, I haven't spoken to him since last Saturday night, so I don't know what's up with him," Stu told them. He couldn't believe that Brett hadn't mentioned he could be moving to Hamilton. Maybe that's why he had called a halt to their experiment-slash-friends with benefits thing. But why hadn't he just come out and said that? Stu would have understood. From what Jase was saying, it sounded like a promotion for Brett, and god knows he deserved it.

"Maybe he's got a new girl?" Sarah suggested. "Maybe he's chatting with her, which is why he doesn't want to hang with you guys." She looked at Stu. "Has he said anything to you, Stu? About a new girlfriend?"

Stu forced a chuckle, trying to hide his disquiet. "If he hasn't said anything to me about Hamilton, what makes you think he's going to tell me about a new girlfriend?"

"True. So, enough about Brett. You met anyone new, Stu?" Sarah asked, dropping into the seat next to him.

"Nah. Haven't been out for a few weeks."

She frowned. "That's not like you."

Stu shrugged. "Eh. Been busy with work, and to be honest, I'm a bit over the clubbing scene. I'm just having a bit of a break."

"Okay, who are you and what have you done with the real Stuart Johnson?" Jase asked, leaning across the table to peer intently at his face. "You look like our Stu, but you don't sound like our Stu."

"Piss off, you idiot." Stu laughed, shoving Jase's face away. "Can't a guy have a break from clubbing and take some time out for himself?"

"Oh my god!" Sarah gasped. "You're growing up! How are we going to live vicariously through you if you become a staid old man?"

"You mean, how are *you* going to live vicariously through Stu," Mike commented, earning a glare from his wife and laughter from the guys.

"Oh, come on. I'm not that bad," Stu protested.

"Yes, you are," Jase shot back. "I've never known you to be with a guy for more than one night, maybe two occasionally."

"Are you implying I'm a man-whore, Jase?" Stu asked, his tone sharpening as the feelings of the last few weeks began to unravel. "Maybe I am, but I'm not sleeping with anyone at the moment and I don't see me sleeping with anyone in the near future, so I'm sorry your source of entertainment has been cut off."

Stu pushed away from the table. He didn't need this shit from his friends. Yes, he had slept with more than an average number of guys, but he was allowed to change. He only wanted one person in his bed now, and he couldn't have him.

"Whoa. I'm only teasing, mate. Although you have to admit, there have been a fair few guys through your bed." Jase reached a hand across the table, a frown marring his features.

"What's going on, Stu?" Sarah asked, laying a gentle hand on his shoulder. "It's not like you to be so defensive."

Stu shrugged her hand off and stood. "Nothing's going on, okay. Maybe I'm just tired of being the butt of the jokes around here. Maybe I am growing up. Maybe you all need to know that I've only slept with three guys since January."

"Stu…"

"Mate…"

Stu shook his head at his friends. "Look, I'm grateful for your concern, and I love you all, but I'm going to go. I'm obviously not great company at the moment." He leaned down and kissed Sarah on the cheek. "Thanks for brunch."

Stu slipped his jacket on and let himself out of the house, leaving a stunned silence behind him.

*****

The buzz of an incoming message had Brett pulling his phone from his pocket.

Charlie: *Hey. Is everything okay with Stu?*

Brett frowned at the screen. Why was Charlie asking him about Stu?

Brett: *What do you mean?*

Charlie: *He was acting weird at brunch.*

Brett: *Weird how?*

Charlie: *He got offended at something J said and stormed out.*

Brett: *What? What did J say?*

Charlie: *Basically called him a man-whore*

Brett re-read the last message again. It wasn't like Jase to call Stu out and it certainly wasn't like Stu to get upset over a comment. He usually shot back with his customary sarcasm.

Brett was unsure how to respond. Regardless of how things were between him and Stu, he was still his best mate and his automatic response was to jump to Stu's defence. He typed out a reply, deleted it, and then typed out another one.

Brett: *Haven't seen him much this week, but I know he's stressed out from work.*

Charlie: *J has messaged to apologise but hasn't heard back.*

Brett: *Give him a few days to cool down. He'll be back to normal in a day or so.*

Charlie: *Ok. See you later this week?*

Brett: *No. Sorry mate. Going to the Mount for Dad's b-day.*

Charlie: *All good. Say hi to your Ma and Pa when you see them.*

Brett sent back a thumbs-up emoji and put his phone away. There was no point trying to message or call Stu to see what had gone on. Stu was avoiding him as much as Brett was evading him. Brett had hoped to hang out with him the day before on his day off, but Stu had left the house early and then disappeared to his room on his return in the evening.

Brett only had himself to blame. He'd started this whole experiment and now things between them were weird and it was affecting the group dynamic.

"Ah, Brett, there you are." The sound of his boss's voice broke into his thoughts.

"What's up, Les?"

"Have you thought any more about what we spoke about a few weeks ago? The job in Hamilton?"

"Ah, sort of," Brett replied sheepishly. He'd avoided thinking about it. Pretty much like everything else he was avoiding thinking about at the moment. *How did my life get so complicated?*

"It would be a great opportunity for you. I know you like it here, but don't think you're letting down the team if you do decide to go. The role down there is quite varied, with a mix of rural and city living," Les told him.

"Yeah, thanks, Les. I'm heading down to the Mount this weekend to see my family, and I'm going to talk to them about it all. Mum's a pretty good sounding board."

"Good idea. It helps to talk about things with someone not involved in the service. Maybe go via Hamilton and check things out while you're passing through. Get a feel for the place."

Brett nodded. "Thanks. I'll see how I'm going for time."

With a smile, Les returned to his office, leaving Brett even more confused than ever.

Chapter Twenty

Brett threw the ball down the beach, and his parents Border Terrier, Bob, took off after it. It was a sunny but cool day in Mt Maunganui, the majestic peak at the end of the beach doing little to block the sea breeze.

"What's up, honey?" his mother asked, nudging his elbow.

"What do you mean?" He'd been expecting the questions all weekend and wasn't really surprised that she was finally asking.

"You've been quiet since you got here on Thursday night. Something is on your mind. A problem shared is a problem halved, you know."

Brett gave her a half grin. Rose Parker liked her sayings. He sighed. He needed to talk to someone and considering his usual go-to person was the one he needed to talk about, he supposed his mother was the next best thing.

"Brett, what is it? You know you can tell me anything."

"Yeah, I know, Mum. I…ah…um…I'm bisexual." He waited for her reaction. Surprise widened her eyes before a loving smile spread across her features.

"I hope you haven't been worrying about coming out, because you know your father and I certainly don't have any issues with how a person identifies."

"No. Actually, that's been the least of my worries," he admitted with a sigh. It was true. His parents had never once given him any reason to think otherwise. They'd always taught tolerance to both him and his sister.

"So, what is worrying you?"

Brett led them over to a bench at the edge of the beach. They sat, and his mum placed a warm hand on his arm.

"I only started questioning my sexuality a couple of months ago and I…I've done a bit of experimenting, and it's been great, but the guy I've been with doesn't do relationships, and I want to be more than friends and…" He broke off and looked her in the eye. "It's so hard, Mum. I think I've fucked up the best thing in my life."

Familiar blue eyes looked searchingly at him. "Why do you think you've mucked everything up?" she asked gently.

"He backed off without explanation after the last time we…y'know." Brett cringed. Oh God, could he be any more embarrassed talking to his mother about his sex life? Where was a tsunami when you needed one?

"Did you say or do something that could have offended him?"

The memory of Stu's gorgeous cock in his mouth had him shuffling in his seat. Stu had certainly seemed into it at the time and had even teased that they'd do it again, but then he'd closed off and they'd barely spoken since.

"No…ah, everything seemed fine at the time." He watched Bob chase after a seagull before daring to glance at his mother. Amusement filled her face, and he rolled his eyes. "You really do like embarrassing me, don't you, Mum?"

Rose chuckled as she gave him a side hug. "It's in my job description, honey." She gave him a nudge. "And then what happened, afterwards?"

"We had dinner, watched TV, and he went all quiet and then, yeah, a few days later I told him we didn't need to carry on with what we were doing and he agreed, but now we haven't spoken in days, and I know he's avoiding me."

His mother just hummed, and Brett watched the waves roll onto the beach as he waited for her advice. After a few minutes of silence, he dragged his attention away from the hypnotic motion and turned to find her looking at him with wide eyes and a look of surprise on her face.

"What?"

"Son, this person you've been experimenting with. Is it Stuart?"

"Ah…um…yeah," he admitted, running a hand around his neck. He gave a short laugh. "Bet you didn't expect that, did you?"

"I suppose if you were ever going to end up with a boyfriend, it would make sense that it was Stuart," she told him.

"We're not boyfriends, Mum. Just, I dunno, friends with benefits? And what do you mean 'it makes sense it's Stu?'"

"You two have always been close, honey. It's not really a surprise that you'd ask him to help you figure out your sexuality or, knowing Stuart, he probably offered, didn't he?"

Brett waggled his hand back and forth. "Fifty-fifty, really."

"Stuart cares deeply for you, Brett. I know he likes to think he's Mr Independent and destined for permanent bachelorhood, but I think, if you talk to him properly, you'll find he just wants to be loved. Of course, he'll have to admit that to himself first." She patted his hand reassuringly. "You and Stuart have fallen out before, honey. I'm sure you can work this out and get back on track."

His mother was going off in tangents, and Brett was struggling to keep up. "What do you mean, Stu and I have fallen out before?"

"Really? Darling, remember when you didn't talk for a month when he started dating that young man from university? You didn't like the guy and barely went to see Stuart. When they broke up, you returned to your old ways."

Brett picked up the ball that Bob had dropped at his feet and hurled it down the beach, watching the small brown dog chase after it with abandon as he mulled over her words.

"I think if you take a good look at your own feelings, you'll know exactly why this is hurting so much." He turned back to his mother to find her looking at him with love and compassion.

"I do care for him, but only as, you know, a mate. Same as I care about Charlie and Jase and the rest of the guys."

"Brett, who is the first person you think of when you want to share news, a joke, a story from work? Who have you spoken to in some form or other nearly every day for the last twenty years? Who is the person you defended when he came out at aged thirteen and got picked on by your soccer team?" Rose placed a hand on Brett's face. "Who is the person you would normally go to with a problem, but can't because he *is* the problem?"

"He's my best mate. Of course I do all those things you just said. Isn't that what best friends do?" he protested hotly.

"True," Rose conceded with a nod, "but you two have always had a deeper connection than any other of your friends. When you were younger, around the time Stu came out, he had such a crush on you. You could see it in the way he watched your every move and how his face lit up when you came in the room. Over the years, as you both got older and went your different ways into the fire service and university, it lessened, but he's always looked at you differently to how he looks at anyone else."

"Why did he never say anything though?" Brett was confused. He'd never noticed that Stu looked at him differently. His mother must be imagining things.

"Self-preservation, I should imagine. If he'd told you he had a crush on you when you were teenagers, would you have stayed friends, or would you have pushed him away?"

"I…I don't know. I'd like to say that it wouldn't have mattered, but honestly, I don't know."

"And if he told you now, that he was possibly in love with you. That he wanted more than whatever it is you've been doing. That maybe he wanted a relationship. What would you say now?"

Brett didn't reply. He thought back to the night he'd last spoken with Stu. When he'd told him he was calling off the experiment. He recalled their conversation and realised that he'd never let Stu speak. Stu had told him he'd been thinking too, and as soon as Brett had said his piece, Stu had left, and he'd not spoken to or seen him since. And then there was the whole walking out of brunch thing.

A chill that had nothing to do with the rising wind went through him. Had his decision upset Stu? Had Stu meant to tell him he wanted more than what they'd been doing?

"Stu has never been a relationship type of guy though, Mum. You know that. I mean, even just a few months ago he stated to all of us that he didn't want love, that he'd leave the relationships to Jase and Kyle and Charlie and Cooper. Why would he change his mind now?" he asked, desperate to understand.

"I don't know, honey. The only person who can answer that is Stuart. But before you talk to him, you need to ask yourself a few questions and sort out your own feelings for him."

Brett nodded. As usual, his mother was right. He'd hoped talking to her would help sort out the mess in his head, but instead it had raised more questions and he was no closer to an answer.

"Is this why you're considering the job in Hamilton?" Rose asked. Brett had told his family about the possibility of moving out of Auckland.

"Maybe? What I said the other night is still true. I can't afford to buy a place in Auckland, and the only way to advance my career is if I move. It's a great opportunity."

"What does Stu say?"

Brett dropped his head to his chest, staring down at his feet. "I haven't told him," he admitted.

"Oh, Brett. Why not?

"I dunno." He shrugged. A jab in his ribs had him looking up at his mother. At her raised eyebrow, he sighed. "Okay, yes, I do. When Les told me about the job, my first thought was '*What about Stu?*' We'd only just started, y'know, fooling around, and I didn't want to leave him."

"And do you want to leave him now?"

Brett shook his head. No, he didn't. He hated the idea of not being near his best mate. A dull ache settled in his chest. *Was this love?* He'd missed Stu since their last conversation. Not only the physical part of things, but hanging out on the couch, teasing him about his poor choices in television viewing. He missed cooking dinner with him. And yes, he missed the physical side. The sex had been some of the best he'd ever had. But they'd not had what Brett thought of as 'full-on sex'.

He'd thought he wouldn't want to bottom, and he knew that Stu didn't like to. Would what they were currently doing be enough? During one of their more explosive blowjobs, Stu's fingers had strayed around his hole and it had added to the whole experience. He'd Googled anal sex and watched some porn and had been turned on by when he'd imagined Stu doing that to him. Of course, then things had gone pear shaped and the subject had become moot. *But was that the reason Stu had backed off? Did he feel that Brett wasn't experienced enough for him and he wanted more?*

"Come on, love. We need to head back. Those look like rain clouds, and I'd rather not be sitting here when it hits."

Brett looked to where his mother was pointing. Calling to Bob, who was exploring the nearby sand banks, they turned towards home.

"Be honest with yourself, Brett. Be honest with Stuart. You can work this out. If it turns out he doesn't want more, then fine, you'll move on, but at least you won't have regrets and always wonder what if?"

Later that night, Brett lay in bed, unable to sleep. He examined every second of the last few months and then further back through the twenty years he'd known Stu. He remembered when they first became friends over a joint science fair project. He'd been excited to be paired with the slightly geeky kid, and when they'd both tried out for the school soccer team, their friendship had developed and deepened.

Stu had spent numerous hours at his house, to the point where Rose had stopped putting the camp bed away as it was used so often for sleepovers. Even being at different high schools hadn't stopped them talking or messaging each other every day. Where one was, the other was rarely far behind.

Even Louise, his most recent girlfriend, had commented on how close he and Stu were. It had been one of her parting shots when she'd told him it was over. She'd fallen for the perceived glamour of having a firefighter for a boyfriend, but the reality of dating a shift worker had soon hit home. On the night of Jase's thirtieth birthday party, she'd told him it was over. She was sick of playing second fiddle to his work and to his friends, that she felt he cared more for Stu than he did for her.

Of course, he denied it, but now, with his mother's words ringing in his ears, he began to second-guess himself. He knew he cared for Stu, as he'd told Rose, but on closer examination, he'd not hurt like this when he and Lou had broken up and he had thought he'd loved her. *Was this love?* Did this heart-wrenching ache that never seemed to go away mean he more than cared for his best friend?

He groaned and buried his head under his pillow as if hiding could make it all go away. *Be honest with yourself,* his mother had said. Shame washed through him. They'd promised honesty and communication, and he'd failed his friend and himself on both counts.

It was time to face facts and see if he could salvage his friendship and relationship with Stu.

Chapter Twenty One

Stu wandered aimlessly around the mall, dodging parents with pushchairs and groups of loud teenagers. He wasn't there for any particular reason other than the need to be out of his house. He needed noise and distraction and had thought he'd find it there, but now that he was looking at the garish window displays and faced with the crowds of people getting a start on their Christmas shopping, he realised it was as bad as being in his quiet, empty house.

With it being just over a month until the holidays, there were decorations up already and large bright colourful piles of merchandise everywhere. He'd decided not to go to the weekly brunch at Sarah and Mike's, still embarrassed by his behaviour the previous week. He'd messaged an apology to the group chat, and all had been forgiven. Noticeable by its absence was the lack of a reply from Brett, but then he'd not been there to see Stu have his mini tantrum.

They had avoided each other all week, and he knew Brett was in Mt Maunganui for his dad's birthday. That was another reason Stu hated all this turmoil—if he lost Brett, he lost his family too. Rose and John Parker had become like parents to him during his teenage years and to not have them in his life would leave a hole.

After being jostled twice in five minutes, Stu decided to leave the crowded mall and head home. If he was going to be miserable, he may as well be miserable from the comfort of his own couch.

As he pulled onto his street, he saw Brett's car in its usual spot in the driveway. Stu frowned and glanced at the clock on his dash. It was only just past lunchtime. He hadn't expected Brett to be home this early. In fact, he'd expected him to be home late evening so as to avoid seeing Stu again.

With a deep breath to calm his jangling nerves, Stu made his way inside. He could hear Brett's low voice coming from the laundry. He paused before pasting a smile on his face then headed to the back of the house.

"Oh, yes, Cap, I know. I've missed you too, but you can't sit there. I need to get these clothes into the washing machine."

Stu grinned as he poked his head into the small utility room where he found his ginger cat demanding head rubs and ear scritches. Stu hungrily drank in the sight of his best friend. He was dressed in old faded jeans and a battered fire department t-shirt which stretched across his broad shoulders. Stu huffed a laugh when Cap swiped at Brett as he tried to lift the furball off the pile of clothing he was perched on.

"Need a hand?" he offered. Brett's head jerked up and a quick grin spread across his features, his eyes bright with amusement.

"Hi. Nah, I'm all good. Young Cap here needs to shift his fuzzy butt so I can get on with my washing."

Stu stepped forward and snagged the cat, who protested loudly before wriggling away. Stu let him drop to the floor and watched him disappear out the cat door with a flick of his tail.

"How was your weekend?" Stu asked, shuffling back to lean against the doorjamb, hands stuffed in pockets of his jeans. "Your dad have a good birthday?"

"It was good, thanks. He says thanks for the card and whisky, by the way, and Mum has sent some cake back for you," Brett said as he quickly loaded the washing machine.

"Is it her world-famous double chocolate?" Stu asked hopefully.

"Sure is. You know that's the only flavour dad eats." Brett grinned.

"I'll make the coffee then," Stu told him and headed into the kitchen. *Okay, this seemed to be going well. They were talking, Brett didn't look like he wanted to run away. They could do this.* He *could do this.*

"So…ah, how's your…um weekend been?"

"Oh, y'know, just mooched about, had a wander around the mall, trying to get inspiration for Christmas," Stu replied, struggling to inject enthusiasm into his tone.

Brett raised an eyebrow at him. "You hate the mall and you do all your shopping last minute online."

"Maybe I've changed. Maybe I've decided to be more organised this year."

"Thanks," Brett said as he took the proffered mug and pushed the container of baking towards Stu. "Change is good."

"Yeah, it is," Stu agreed softly, busying himself with the cake so he didn't have to look at his friend.

A muffled curse and the sound of Brett's mug coming down heavily on the kitchen counter had Stu looking up, startled. He barely had time to put the knife down before being pushed back against the cupboard and Brett's mouth was on his, tongue sweeping against his lips, forcing him to open up.

Stu wasn't sure who groaned, but he met Brett's onslaught with his own. The bitter tang of coffee gave way to Brett's unique taste. Stu wrapped his arms around Brett, pulling him closer as heat raced through his veins.

"God, I've missed this." Brett's voice was hoarse as he kissed along Stu's jaw before biting gently on his earlobe. "Why did I want to stop this?" he muttered, pressing his groin into Stu's hip.

Some of the heat dissipated from Stu at the words and he pushed against the firm chest pressing against him.

"Wait, stop, B," he pleaded as a shiver went through him at the scrape of stubble against his throat.

"Don't wanna stop. You taste so fucking good. I want to kiss you all over," Brett whispered against his lips before kissing him again. Stu lost himself in the kiss for a few seconds, before reasoning took over. Brett hadn't missed him, just their physical interactions. *No, I won't do this. I need some answers. I need to tell Brett how I feel.*

Stu ripped his mouth away while simultaneously pushing Brett's chest. As soon as he could move, he stepped aside from Brett, trying not to notice the hurt and disappointment in the other man's eyes.

"What's going on, B?" At Brett's raised eyebrow, Stu lifted a hand. "And, no, I don't mean the kiss. I am very aware you were kissing me. What I need to know is why? Two weeks ago, you decided you wanted to stop the sex and now you're all over me after not speaking to me since. What gives?"

Brett ran his fingers through his hair before his shoulders slumped and he let out a sigh. "If we're going to do this, we may as well be comfortable." He led the way into the lounge and dropped onto his usual corner of the couch.

Stu followed slowly behind him, unsure of what would happen next. He tried to tamp down the ember of hope starting to glow inside him. It was time to tell Brett he was ready for a relationship. He only hoped Brett was thinking the same.

*****

Brett internally kicked himself for jumping Stu. But, dammit, his friend looked so damn good, and after two weeks of not being able to touch him, Brett couldn't help himself. He watched as Stu settled on the opposite end of the couch, a wary expression on his face.

Brett didn't blame him. He'd be wary too if someone he'd pushed away was suddenly all over him like a rash. After lying awake most of the night, he'd left straight after breakfast, a knowing look on his mother's face as she'd hugged him goodbye.

"You going to stare at the floor all day or are you going to talk?" Stu asked.

"Sorry. You're right." Brett closed his eyes and gathered his courage. He turned to face his best friend. The man that had been there for him for over twenty years. He took in the familiar features of always stylishly cut dirty blond hair, denim-blue eyes currently absent of their usual sparkle of amusement. He noticed the faint shadows under those eyes and the slightly pinched mouth, signs of stress Stu was trying so hard to hide. The stress he had contributed to, and his heart broke for the man he loved.

Yes, he'd finally admitted that he was in love with Stuart. Not just like a brother or best mate, but all encompassing, can't-live-without-him love.

"I had a big talk with Mum yesterday. Told her I was bisexual."

"How'd she take that?"

"How do you think?" Brett replied with a snort.

"Let me guess, there's a rainbow flag hanging on the wall and she's on the organising committee for Mt Maunganui's first Pride parade?"

Brett laughed, the tension easing slightly with Stu's teasing.

"I imagine she's co-chair," he said through his laughter. Sobering, he looked his friend in the eye. "Why did you agree so easily to let me experiment with you?"

Stu dropped his gaze to his lap, and Brett saw how he twisted his fingers together. A rare sign that Stu was nervous. "Stu, please, I need to know."

"I don't know. You sort of sprung it on me that you wanted to try being with a guy, and that first kiss… I don't know." Stu sighed, his voice tapering off.

"Mum told me you used to have a crush on me, y'know, when we were kids," Brett said. At his words, Stu's head flew up, eyes wide.

"She wh…what?"

"She said you had a crush on me, back when you came out," Brett repeated. Watching carefully, he asked, "Did you? Is that why you were happy to let me experiment with you?"

A dull flush rose on Stu's face and he dropped his gaze away again. "Maybe." He shrugged.

Brett waited for more, but Stu was silent. Bucky wandered in and jumped onto the couch between them, settling onto the cushion, oblivious to the tension in the room.

"Maybe? Is that all? Maybe what? Maybe you had a crush on me, or maybe it was why you happily let me experiment with you because you still have feelings for me?"

"What do you want from me, B? I don't know, all right? You're my best mate, the guy that's been like a brother to me. I know I care about you a lot. It just felt *right* when we kissed. I just… I just don't know." Stu's voice tapered off to a quiet whisper, and he still wouldn't look at Brett.

"I do know, Stu. I know because it's the same for me."

"What do you mean?" Stu finally looked at Brett, confusion in his eyes.

"I mean that I care about you too. I always have. Like you said, we've been like brothers and I can't imagine not having you in my life. Mum told me I needed to be honest with myself, and with you." He huffed out a laugh. "Hardly got any sleep last night for thinking about everything. Thinking about you and how much you mean to me."

"And what conclusion did you come to?" Stu eyed him warily.

"That I'm glad we're not brothers."

"Oh." Stu looked crestfallen at Brett's statement.

"I'm glad we're not brothers because what we've been doing would be wrong on *so* many levels." Brett was pleased to see the corner of Stu's mouth lift slightly. He took a deep breath. "And I don't love you like a brother."

Confusion raced across Stu's face before it was hidden behind a stony mask.

"What? Are you saying you think you love me because we got off with each other a few times?" Stu huffed out. "You're just confused and mistaking lust and being horny for something that's not real."

"Why'd you get shitty at brunch last weekend?" Brett fired back, hurt that his feelings were being dismissed so easily. He knew being on the defensive was Stu's default setting when he was cornered, but it didn't make it hurt any less.

Stu shrugged and shook his head. "I was tired, I snapped at something Jase said. It was nothing."

"Wanna know what I think," Brett started but was interrupted.

"Oh, go on. Yes, tell me what you think. No wait, let me guess. You think I snapped because Jase called me a man-whore and I took it personally. You think just because you and I have been sleeping together, that I haven't been with another guy in weeks, that somehow, I suddenly have feelings for you that go beyond friends."

Watching his friend get all steamed up, his colour heightened, eyes shining defensively, melted something inside Brett and he couldn't help a small smile.

"What? What the fuck are you smiling at? Am I a joke to you?" Stu stood, throwing his hands in the air. "Of course, I am. This is all a fucking joke. Well, you can take your jokes, your supposed feelings, and all your crap and go. Pack up your stuff and just go, Brett. I'm sure Charlie will let you stay in one of the cottages until you move to Hamilton." Stu paused for a breath. "And that's another fucking thing. When were you going to tell me you were moving to Hamilton? How come I had to hear it from Jase?"

"You want me to go? You want me to move out?" Brett froze in place, his mind latching onto the one phrase he hadn't expected to hear. This was *so* not going how he'd thought it would.

"You may as well. It's not like you want to 'experiment' anymore. You know you're bi. Maybe you'll find a nice guy or girl in your new hometown." Stu sneered back.

"I don't want a nice guy or girl from Hamilton, or anywhere else for that matter. I only want *you*!" Brett was on his feet now.

"Oh, so now you're saying I'm not nice. Great! Don't let the door hit you on the way out!"

Brett rolled his eyes and grabbed at Stu before he could storm out. His friend glared at him and pulled his arm free. Brett raised his hands in surrender. "Stu, please, babe. Stop. Please, just stop," he said wearily. He didn't want to fight. He just wanted to hold him and love him. Convince the stubborn ass that they could have a relationship.

"Did you just call me babe?"

"What? Don't you like it?" Brett reached for Stu's hand, only to have him pull away again.

Disappointment washed through him. This had all been a mistake. "I'm sorry, Stu. Sorry for everything. I'll start packing my gear up and head over to Charlie's tonight. I'll…um…grab the rest at the end of the week when I'm off shift."

He moved towards the door, his feet heavy. He glanced back at Stu, who was still standing by the couch, his face a blank mask. "Thanks. For everything. You'll always be my best friend, Stu. I ho-hope we can still be friends." He swallowed, trying to keep his emotions in check. He'd never thought it would come to this. He'd been a fool to think otherwise.

Chapter Twenty-Two

Stu stood frozen in the middle of his lounge, watching as his best friend walked away. *What was he doing? This had all gone so wrong!*

When Brett had said he didn't love him like a brother, hope had flared momentarily. Instead of calmly responding, he'd automatically jumped to deny any possibility of real feelings between them. His fear of being rejected again had kicked in and he'd fired back without thought or care.

After his walk out at brunch last week, he'd realised that things were never going to be the same between him and Brett ever again. They'd crossed the friend line, and being alone in the house had made him face certain truths about himself. A night of self-pity involving a bottle of wine and a pizza had him admitting that he loved Brett.

He wanted to believe that maybe Brett did care for him more than just as a friend but was sure the other man's feelings were a result of finally being free sexually. And then his friend had called him babe. In all the years Brett had dated, he had never, ever, called his lover by a pet name. In fact, he teased Jase and Kyle about their pet names for each other. It just wasn't something that Brett did.

"B, wait. Why'd you call me babe?" he asked. He didn't know why it was so important that he know the answer, but it was. There were more important things to be discussed, but he needed to know.

"I dunno. Just slipped out. Sorry. Won't happen again, obviously." The last word of that sentence was a mumble.

"You've never called anyone babe before, so why'd you say it to me?" Stu pushed, a glimmer of hope rising in him.

"I said I don't know, Stu. I'm sorry, okay? Heat of the moment." Brett's voice rose in frustration and his eyes shimmered brightly. *Was…was Brett close to tears?*

"You were right," Stu said in a rush. He couldn't let Brett go without telling him the truth. Not if he wanted any semblance of a relationship in the future, whether it be as friends or lovers.

"Right about what?"

"I…I…did have a crush on you when we were kids. And I do have feelings for you now."

Brett stared at him from the doorway, face impassive.

"Can we start this conversation again? Please?" Stu motioned to the couch and held his breath for a moment until Brett gave a small nod and made his way back to sit down.

They sat in silence as Stu gathered his thoughts. Brett looked like he was going to get up again, and Stu held out a staying hand.

"Hold on. Just give me a sec. This is harder than I thought it would be." He took a deep breath and looked at Brett.

"Hi, my name is Stuart, and I'm an idiot," he began. Brett gave a small smirk, and Stu smiled back at him. "I'm in love with my best friend and I don't know how to tell him. I don't know how to tell him I was wrong about relationships. That they aren't the big scary thing I had to run from. I don't know how to tell him that the last couple of weeks without him in my life have been miserable and that the kids at school have started to call me Jerk-Face Johnson behind my back because I've taken my frustrations out on them." Stu paused, licking his dry lips. "I know you don't feel the same way, but I hope we can continue what we started and maybe see how it goes from there."

The surrounding air was still, the only sound the rustle of the trees outside. They stared at each other, and Stu was starting to worry that he'd read things wrong.

"I don't know why I called you babe. Like everything else over the last few weeks, it just felt right. It felt natural," Brett told him, his eyes searching Stu's face. Stu nodded in encouragement. "And you're right, you are an idiot, but you're also wrong. I do feel the same way. I love you, Stu. We've probably loved each other for years. Who knows? What I do know is that when I kissed you that first time, it lit a spark in me. I've never felt like this before. I know I've cared for my previous lovers, thought that I loved them, but with you it's been different."

"I should bloody well hope so," Stu said, unable to resist teasing a little now that the tension had eased. Brett rolled his eyes, and they grinned at each other.

"So what happens now?" Stu asked.

"Right now we're going to go to your bedroom so I can show you how much I love you. Then we'll figure it out as we go."

"Are you sure, B? Are you sure this is what you want?"

"Yes, Stu. I'm sure. I want you. In every way I can have you."

Stu raised an eyebrow. "*Every* way?"

A blush stained Brett's cheek as he moved across the couch. "Is that a deal breaker? I know you've said it doesn't matter, but that was short term. If we're going to do this whole relationship thing, is it going to be a problem if we don't do anal?"

Stu reached up and pulled Brett's face closer. He placed a light kiss on his lips before drawing back. "No, it's not a deal breaker. I want you any way you want to give yourself to me. And besides, there is so much more for me to teach you."

"If I change my mind, will you teach me that too?" Brett asked quietly.

"I…of course," Stu hadn't been expecting that. Curiosity had him asking, "Do you think you'll change your mind?"

"Maybe? I kind of liked it when you played down there that last time you gave me a blowjob," Brett admitted, dropping his gaze.

Stu smiled and cupped Brett's chin. "This has always been your experiment, B. I'll go at whatever pace you like, as long as I'm doing it with you." He leaned in for a kiss, gently probing until Brett relaxed under his touch.

They sank into the couch, unconsciously arranging themselves until they fit together like puzzle pieces. Stu ran his hands down Brett's spine and over the curve of his arse. He loved the way the muscles tensed and flexed under his touch as Brett rolled his hips, trying to simultaneously rub himself against Stu's thigh and push into the hands caressing him.

Stu dragged his hands slowly up Brett's body, snagging the edge of his t-shirt and pulling it up until Brett broke away long enough to rip it over his head before returning his mouth to Stu's. Stu traced along the warm skin of Brett's shoulders then down his spine and back up again, reacquainting himself with every dip and curve.

He slid his mouth along Brett's stubble-roughened jaw before nibbling down his neck to where it met his shoulder. He inhaled deeply, drawing the familiar scent into his lungs. His fingers tangled in the silky softness of Brett's hair, and he gently pulled the other man up so he could stare into the face that was so familiar and meant so much to him.

"I've missed you," Brett murmured, tenderness shining from his eyes, a small smile lighting his features.

"I've really missed you, too," Stu replied. "Not just this"—he nodded to how close they were pushed together—"but everything. Talking to you, texting you, even just hanging out watching TV."

"What made you realise that relationships weren't the big scary thing you though they were?" Brett asked as he cradled Stu's jaw with a gentle hand.

Stu leaned briefly into the caress before turning to press a kiss against the pulse beating in Brett's wrist. "When I realised we'd been in a relationship pretty much since that first kiss. I always thought that I'd hate having to change my ways to accommodate someone else's wants and needs into my life. But you just fit in, and with your shifts, I get the best of both worlds."

"What do you mean the best of both worlds?" A frown creased Brett's brow, and Stu gave him a quick kiss before grinning at him.

"I mean, I get to spend time with a gorgeous, hot fireman, who not only knows all my quirks and secrets, but respects them, and then I get my alone time when you're on shift."

"You really think I'm gorgeous and hot?"

Stu nodded. "And kind. Generous. Thoughtful. Sexy. Strong." Stu punctuated each word with a kiss. "And even more importantly, mine."

Brett grinned at the last statement. "Look at you, all possessive. I like it." He lowered his head, and as their lips brushed, he muttered, "and you're mine too." The kiss was tender, loving and, yes, possessive as both of them imparted their feelings for the other.

They were settling into a heavy make-out session when Stu's phone rang, bursting them out of the bubble they were in.

"Ignore it," Brett mumbled as he rutted against Stu's thigh. The ring tone stopped briefly before starting again. "Fuuuckk! Who the hell wants to talk to you so badly?"

"Dunno, but it may be important." Stu reluctantly pushed Brett away enough to stretch out to grab his phone off the coffee table. He glanced at the caller ID and rolled his eyes as he swiped to accept the call.

"Hi, Jase. What's up?" Stu frowned as Brett stood and headed for the kitchen. "What? Yes. Sorry. Yes, I'm at home." His gaze fixed on Brett's arse, and he struggled to focus on what Jase was saying to him. "Oh. You're coming over. When? Now? Oh, yeah. Sure. That's fine. See you soon. Okay. Bye." He disconnected the call and dropped his phone onto the table.

"B, Jase and Kyle are on their way over," he called out.

"What? Why?" Brett asked as he came back into the lounge with a glass of water.

"I don't know." Stu sighed. "I think Jase is still feeling bad about last week and wants to talk." He gave a small pout as Brett pulled his shirt back on.

Brett grinned at the look. "Later, babe. You can see it again later." He winked and waved a hand down his body. "In fact, you can see it all later."

"What are we going to tell the guys?" He took Brett's hand in his as he dropped onto the couch next to him. "Are you ready to go public? What about work? This is a big thing, B. People will look at you differently. Are you ready for that?"

Brett sighed and ran his free hand across his face. "Yeah. I know. I think I'm just going to play it by ear. Take it on a case-by-case situation."

"Okay. Whatever you decide is fine by me. It's your news to share as you see fit. You don't owe anyone any explanations."

"I know. Telling my family was okay, but telling the guys"—he shook his head—"They're going to give me *so* much shit."

"I know they are, but think of it this way. If you were introducing anyone else as your boyfriend, it would have been *me* giving you the most shit, so at least you've got lucky that way."

Brett side-eyed him and sighed again. "Go on, say it. I know you're dying to."

Stu cackled and straddled Brett's lap, cradling his face in his hands and staring deeply into the dark blue eyes. "I told you so!" he crowed before kissing him briefly. "I told you that if you came over to my side of the fence, you'd love it. I told you that all you needed was to be shown how good being with a guy could be."

"Ah, but I haven't come over to your side of the fence. I'm sitting on it, aren't I?" Brett countered, and although he smiled, Stu could see an emotion he couldn't name in his eyes.

"Oh, B. You can stand, sit, jump on anywhere you want. Being bisexual is a valid thing. Just because right now, at this time, the person you are attracted to, that you want to be with, happens to be male rather than a female, is okay. I think you've always known you probably were attracted to both sexes, but you've never acted on it. Whatever triggered your subconscious to act on it now, who cares? All I care about is that you're comfortable with it all. That you're okay and comfortable with us. Everyone else can go jump."

"I love you, Stuart Edward Johnson."

Stu grinned. "And I love you, Brett Dean Parker. Now, I'm going to tidy myself up before Jase and Kyle get here." He ran an eye over Brett's dishevelled appearance. "And you may want to do the same, otherwise they'll guess before you get a chance to tell them."

They kissed briefly before heading to their respective rooms. Stu felt lighter than he had in days. In fact, probably lighter than he'd ever been. He knew they still had things to work out, and telling their friends was the first big hurdle. The guys might tease Brett for succumbing, but it would be nothing like the shit he was going to get for finally falling in love and wanting a relationship.

Chapter Twenty-Three

Brett looked in the mirror at the mess that was his hair. He needed a haircut, but it would have to wait until his next day off. He ran a hand through the tousled strands and decided the only way to get them to lie down would be to shower. He grabbed a fresh t-shirt from his drawer and headed to the bathroom.

"Stu, I'm just going to grab a quick shower," he called down the hallway. Stu's head popped around his bedroom door, and the look of heat he gave had Brett wishing their friends weren't on their way over.

"Thanks, B. Now I'll be imagining you all naked and wet. I've only just got myself under control," Stu grumbled, but Brett could see he was teasing.

"If it's any consolation, it'll now be a cold one," he replied with a wink before shutting the door on Stu's laughter.

Ten minutes later he gave himself a quick once over. He looked tidier and the shower had not only cooled his libido but taken some of the heated flush out of his face. He heard a knock at the front door and took a breath before leaving his room. It was show time.

As he walked into the lounge, it surprised him to see that, along with Kyle and Jase, the rest of the gang were there too. He flicked a glance at Stu, who managed a discreet shrug before asking everyone for their drink preferences.

Brett shook hands with his friends and gave Sarah a brief hug and kiss on the cheek. She stared at him for a lengthy moment before nodding to herself. Brett wasn't sure what that was all about, but, knowing Sarah, he was certain to find out before long.

"So, what's the occasion?" Stu asked as he returned to the room with a tray of hot drinks. Brett took his coffee mug and sat on the couch. There was some shuffling and murmurs before Jase cleared his throat.

"There's no easy way to say this. Stu, we're worried about you, mate."

Stu sat up straighter from his position at the opposite end of the couch. "Worried? About me? Why?"

Jase perched himself on the edge of the coffee table in front of Stu. "You've seemed down lately. We know you like to keep yourself to yourself, but you've really closed off these last few weeks, and we want you to know, whatever it is, we're here to help in any way we can."

Brett buried his nose in his mug to prevent from laughing out loud. From the corner of his eye he saw Stu glance at him, and he deliberately averted his gaze and noticed that Cooper was watching him with an inscrutable expression. Brett gave a half smile and focused back on the conversation.

"Look, everything is fine. Honestly. Yes, I've been a bit down. I've had a few things on my mind and I just needed to work through them. I didn't mean to worry you all."

"Hmm, if you're sure?" Jase didn't sound convinced. At Stu's nod, Jase accepted what his friend had said before turning his dark green eyes on Brett. "And what's going on with you, Brett?"

"Me? Nothing,"

"You sure? Have you made a decision about Hamilton yet?" Kyle asked from where he was sitting in the armchair.

Brett flicked at a glance at Stu before returning his attention to Kyle. He and Stu hadn't got that far in their discussions, having gotten side-tracked with making out.

"Ah. Um. Yeah. Sort of." He needed to discuss this with Stu before he spoke about it with anyone else, but it didn't look like he would get the opportunity.

"What I want to know is, what's so good about Hamilton when you have everything here?" Sarah commented.

"Yeah, B. What's Hamilton got that you want to move?" Stu asked, and Brett whipped around to stare at him.

"What the fuck?" he breathed out, disbelief and hurt rushing through him at Stu's question. Was he serious? Did Stu really not want him after all? After all they'd said to each other today. Had it been a lie?

He glared at his best friend, who just raised an eyebrow back at him. Brett was about to storm out when he saw the familiar glint of amusement in Stu's eyes. *Right. So that's how he wanted to play this.* Brett set his coffee mug down and angled his body towards Stu's, crossing his arms.

"Hamilton has lots of great things going for it, including a promotion and better house prices. Why should I stay in Auckland?"

A brief flash of alarm crossed Stu's features before he drew himself up taller. "What about your friends? What about us?" he asked, sweeping an arm to encompass everyone in the room.

"Oh, for fucks sake!" Sarah broke in, exasperated. "When are you two going to finally admit you're sleeping with each other?"

All eyes turned towards her. "What are you talking about?" Charlie asked.

Brett watched as Sarah looked at them all and rolled her eyes. "Honestly? It figures. I suppose if you lot had worked out they were having sex, this intervention would have taken place a long time ago and Brett wouldn't be thinking about moving to Hamilton and Stu wouldn't be such a grumpy bastard."

"Hang on, I'm lost. Brett's straight." Mike sounded confused and looked to his wife. "Isn't he?"

"That's something only Brett, and probably Stu, can answer, honey," Sarah replied.

"Actually, the bigger question is, when are they going to admit they love each other and have done for years?" Cooper said.

"True, but I thought I'd lead with the sex question. More entertaining to see their reactions," she said with a grin.

"Wait. How come you think they love each other?" Charlie asked his fiancée. "You've only known them a few months.

"Exactly. You guys have been around them so long, you don't notice how they mirror each other, how they act and react to each other. It's just normal behaviour to you. I saw it pretty much straight away when I first met them. Sarah confirmed it for me one day before I went back to England." Sarah nodded in agreement at Cooper's statement.

"So, is it true?" Jase asked, turning his attention back to Brett and Stu. They glanced at each other, and Stu shrugged. Brett sighed. He knew what Stu was trying to tell him. It was his news to tell.

"Which part?" he stalled.

"All of it!" Jase said. "Are you sleeping together and are you in love with each other, and if you are, when did it all happen?"

"God, you don't want much, do you?" Brett said.

"We want to know that you two are okay. We've noticed you've both been avoiding each other for weeks now. You keep staying out at Charlie's on your days off, which makes me think maybe things aren't are simple as Cooper and Sarah seem to think they are," Jase said, concern in his eyes.

Brett knew they cared. He would have been the same if the tables were turned. He decided, though, to spin them out a bit longer. Served them right for being nosy. He turned to Stu.

"Stu, is it true? Do you love me?" he asked and bit back a smile when Stu's eyes widened and then narrowed as he figured out what Brett was doing.

"I love all of you," Stu said airily, darting a glance around the room. "What about you? Do you love me?"

"Sometimes. Y'know, when you're not hogging the TV remote or when you're doing that thing." Brett tried not to grin.

"Thing? What thing… oh, *that* thing. Well, of course you love me when I do *that* thing," Stu said, his eyes dancing with amusement.

Charlie eyed him suspiciously as Cooper snorted with laughter and tried unsuccessfully to calm himself. "Good on ya, lads," he got out between sniggers.

Brett couldn't help himself and started to laugh too, which caused Stu to join in. The others looked at them like they'd gone mad. After a moment to collect himself, Brett smiled at his friends. "Okay. Here's the thing. I've recently figured out I'm bisexual and, yes, Stu has been helping me with that."

"How?" Mike asked, still confused.

"By doing the *thing*," Sarah said as she swatted her husband's arm. "Honestly, babe, keep up."

"But what's the 'thing'?" Mike asked her, rubbing his arm. Sarah rolled her eyes.

"I'm guessing it's with his tongue," Kyle said with a smirk.

"Well, one of them is," Brett said, giving a filthy wink. Mike looked at Brett, then at Stu, and then back to

Brett. A dull stain coloured Mike's face as he realised what was being said.

"Oooh, has he got more than one trick then?" Sarah asked gleefully.

"Sarah, darling, you should know better than that," Stu drawled. "I know *all* the tricks."

"Okay, TMI. We don't need to know about your tricks," Jase said, trying to steer the conversation back on track. "So, you're bi, Brett. When did you realise?"

Brett settled back into the couch. "A couple of months ago. Nothing specific happened, I just got curious—"

"And drunk," Stu interjected.

"All right, yes, and drunk, and one thing led to another and we started…um…experimenting and, yeah…that's about it."

"And when did you figure out you're in love with each other?" Sarah asked, her curiosity getting the better of her.

"About twenty-four hours ago," Brett admitted, casting a warm glance towards Stu. Stu blushed and dropped his gaze.

"And you, Stu, when did you realise?" Sarah nudged.

"About three weeks ago," he said softly, and Brett's heart lurched.

"Wait. Three weeks ago? Why didn't you say something?" he asked as his brain tracked along the timeline. Three weeks? "Oh shit. The night I called it all off. You were going to tell me then, weren't you?"

Stu shrugged, and Brett could see he wasn't comfortable talking about this with their friends around. Brett stretched a hand across the couch and grabbed Stuart's. "I'm sorry. I didn't realise."

"S'okay. We've figured it out now, that's the main thing."

"Okay, guys. Time to go." Sarah stood and made shooing motions with her hands. "These guys need some privacy. They've got a lot to work out." The others all quickly stood, and there was a flurry of handshakes and promises of getting together soon.

"Remember, we're here if you need anything," Sarah told them both as she gave them a warm hug. "I'm so happy for you. Love you both."

Brett pushed the door shut on their friends and eyed Stu where he was standing at the end of the hall.

"So, that happened," he said as he slowly stalked towards his lover.

"It did. What happens now?" Stu asked as he met him halfway.

"We go in there and pick up where we left off before our well-meaning but meddling friends rudely interrupted us," Brett said, nodding towards Stuart's bedroom.

Stu wound his arms around Brett's neck and pulled him into a kiss. Brett settled his hands on Stu's hips, tugging him closer.

"We still have lots to talk about, to figure out," he said as they broke for air.

"I know we do. But tell me first, what about Hamilton? I don't want you to miss out on a promotion because of me. I'd never hold you back like that."

"I know you wouldn't. It's only a possibility at the moment, and only if I apply for it. Nothing is going to happen this side of the New Year, and honestly, I was only considering it because I couldn't face being here in Auckland and not having you in my life. There'll be other opportunities for promotion, but there won't be another opportunity to be with the man I love. So, I'm sorry, but you're stuck with me."

"Okay then. Now get in there and strip. We have some catching up to do."

With a laugh, Brett let himself be pushed into the waiting bedroom.

Epilogue

The echoing bass pounded through the speakers as the crowd in The Smoking Keg danced and partied the night away. It was only a week before Christmas and people were out celebrating the upcoming holiday with friends and work colleagues.

Stu, Brett, and their friends were having one last get together before they got caught up in family holiday plans. Kyle's family would arrive from Texas in a few days' time, and Cooper's mum and sisters had landed earlier in the week. Twins Saskea and Sofia were out on the dancefloor while Carl, Charlie's brother and Cooper's bodyguard, kept a close eye on them.

People in the bar had pretty much ignored the fact they had a major celebrity in their midst, their attention initially being split between Cooper and Reuben Taylor, the first openly gay All Black, who was out with his partner, Cam. Stu had teased Brett for being starstruck when he'd spotted the sportsman from across the room.

Brett finished his beer and grabbed Stu by the hand. "Come on," he half shouted to be heard over the noise. "I know you're dying to get out there and dance."

Stu grinned at him and let himself be led into the heaving mass of bodies. It was hot and humid and sticky, but it didn't stop Stu plastering himself against Brett and letting his body grind in time to the music. Brett's hands settled on his arse, pulling him in closer to nuzzle at his neck.

Stu was pleasantly surprised at the public display of affection. This was their first real outing as a couple, and he was relieved Brett was comfortable enough to be himself. At home, Brett had moved into Stu's bed, and they had fallen into a routine of happy domesticity.

Stuart had informed his parents about the change in his relationship with his oldest friend and, as expected, they had made some bland comment and then told Stu they would be in the UK for the next eight weeks and they'd see him on their return. Brett's parents, of course, had been all hugs and told Stu they'd always considered him part of the family and now it was official.

There had been the predicted teasing from their friends, and Jase had admitted it was strange to have them together as a couple rather than as mates, but they were all slowly getting used to the new normal.

"Brett, is that you?" a voice interrupted their slow grind, and Stu glanced up to find a younger man with a big grin standing next to Brett.

"Chalky, mate. Good to see you," Brett said, untangling himself from Stu to shake the other man's hand.

Chalky's gaze darted between the two of them. Brett huffed a laugh. "Stu, this is Chalky, from work. Chalky, this is Stu, my boyfriend." A thrill went through Stu at being called boyfriend and he grinned as they shook hands.

"Thought you said you were straight?" Chalky said with a nod to them both.

"Yeah. Maybe not so much," Brett admitted with a fond look at Stu.

"Good on ya," Chalky said. "Anyway, have a good night. See you at work next week."

Brett waved goodbye before pulling Stu back into his arms.

"I think your friend is disappointed that you didn't tell him you were bi," Stu said.

"Wouldn't have mattered. The only bloke I want is right here, in front of me," Brett told him before kissing him slowly.

"Oi, get a room, you two." Jase's amused voice broke them apart.

Brett gave his mate the finger before asking Stu if he was ready to go. Stu nodded, and with a hug to Jase and Kyle, they made their way back to the small roped off VIP area where Charlie and Cooper were talking to the owner of the bar. They said their goodbyes and headed out into the cooler air.

Brett ordered an Uber and he and Stu made their way from the pedestrian only area of Auckland's Viaduct harbour towards the road.

They stood shoulder to shoulder while they waited for their ride, Brett glancing at his phone periodically to track its whereabouts.

"Five more minutes," he said, throwing an arm around Stu's shoulders.

A group of women passed by them, giggling and stumbling as they made their way towards one of the other bars. Stu watched as Brett ran an eye over them before returning his attention back to his phone.

"Anyone take your fancy?" he asked, nodding towards the women.

"What?" Brett looked up, glancing towards where Stu was nodding and then back at him.

"Any of the girls take your fancy?" Stu asked again, curious to see how Brett would answer. He was confident in their relationship, but something made him ask.

"You're kidding, right?" Brett asked. "I'll admit they're an attractive group, and if I was a single man, I may be tempted to ask one of them for a drink. But I am not a single man. I am very much in love with my best friend, and if he thinks I would even look at another person, male or female, while I am with him, then maybe he doesn't really know me after twenty years of friendship."

The appearance of their ride stopped Stu from making an immediate response. He waited until they were in the car before twining his fingers with Brett's. "I'm sorry. That was stupid of me. I do know you better than that."

Brett smirked at him. "You can make it up to me when we get home."

"Do you have any suggestions on what I can do to make it up to you?" Stu teased back, happy to see Brett wasn't mad at him.

"I do. We'll start with you slowly removing all my clothes," Brett whispered, leaning towards him so the driver wouldn't hear them.

"Mmm hmm," Stu hummed in agreement, his fingers tracing lazy circles on Brett's thigh.

"And then you can do all the washing and ironing for the rest of the week."

Stu gave him a flat stare. "You really need to work on your seduction technique. Have you learned nothing from me?"

"I've learned that you're a terrible tease in bed, and that tonight I will get my own back."

"How?"

"I'm going to edge you until you beg for release, and then I'll make you come so hard, you can't remember what day of the week it is," Brett told him.

Stu groaned softly and shifted in his seat, trying to ease the pressure in his jeans. "Fucking flirt," he growled.

"I learnt from the master, or so he tells me."

Stu was relieved when they pulled onto their street. With a hurried thanks to their driver, they rushed into the house.

It didn't take them but a moment to strip, and soon he was writhing under Brett's touch. As promised, Brett teased and taunted him with his mouth and hands, and it wasn't long before Stu was shouting his torturer's name in ecstasy.

As they recovered and slowly drifted towards sleep, Brett asked, "You weren't really worried earlier, were you? Y'know, when the girls walked past."

"No, B, I wasn't," Stu replied sleepily. He snuggled closer into Brett's back, pressing a warm kiss to the nape of his neck. "I know you love me, as much as I love you. It's normal to look, but I know you'll never cheat. It's not in your makeup to do that."

"I love you, Stu. You're my everything, and I just wish we'd figured it out earlier."

"Nah. We weren't meant to be together until now. We're right where we're supposed to be."

And they were.

The End

****

Bonus scene

Want to read about Cooper's proposal to Charlie?

Sign up to my newsletter to read this short bonus scene

https://mailchi.mp/674e96d5817c/true-north

****

About the Author

Zoe Piper is English by birth and a Kiwi by choice, living in Auckland, New Zealand for over thirty years. By day she is an international arms dealer, (yes, really), mother to two horrible teenage boys and long-suffering partner of their father. She has been reading since she learned the alphabet as a small child and devours several books a week. She loves a good romance and a happy ever after. She began reading about boys falling in love with boys after a recommendation from a good friend.

Zoe is a member of Romance Writers New Zealand (RWNZ) and placed second in the 2019 Koru Award for Excellence - Long Romance with her novel, The Sweetest Song.

You can keep in touch with Zoe on social media

Facebook:

Zoe Piper - https://www.facebook.com/zoe.piper.5680

Author page - https://www.facebook.com/ZoePiperAuthor/

Reader Groups :

Zoe's Chatter Box - https://www.facebook.com/groups/ZoesChatterBox

Kiwi Authors Rainbow Readers - https://www.facebook.com/groups/KiwiAuthorsRainbowReaders/

Newsletter: - https://mailchi.mp/ba4a6d6cb20b/zoepiperauthor

Email: zoepiperauthor@gmail.com